MOLLY LEARNS TO FLOAT

A novel by Diane Wade

This is a work of fiction. Names, characters, places and incidents either are used fictitiously or are the products of the author's imagination. Any resemblance to actual persons, living or dead, events or locales are coincidental.

Introduction

Molly's story is loosely based on the challenges I faced after the sudden loss of my husband of 35 years. But her storyline, the people in it, and her specific experiences in this new chapter of life are all her own.

My goal in writing this book is to hopefully inspire a woman or two that even at almost 60, when you may feel you are becoming invisible, it is possible to find beauty in life again and flourish, even after devastating tragedy.

Dedication

This book is dedicated, with special thanks to:
- my love Dan for his never-ending enthusiasm, support and encouragement that helped convince me to write this book.
- my amazing daughters who inspire me every day in their ability to face life's challenges with optimism and good humor.
- and in loving memory always of Dave.

Table of Contents

SIXTY IS THE NEW....21?!	6
BACKSTORY	9
AFTER THE FUNERAL	14
BABY STEPS	17
DARBY'S WORLD	20
ROBBIE AND LIZZIE	28
THE MAKEOVER	30
GUILTY FEELINGS	36
SPIRITUAL HELP	38
GETTING OUT THERE	41
THE REAL WORLD GUY	44
INTERNET FIRSTS: FROM MR. KINKY SENSE OF HUMOR TO MR. WEEBLE.	51
FAMILY LIFE REINVENTED	54
THE FRIENDLY POLICE OFFICER:	58
NOT REAL. NOT FUNNY.	66
VERY BLIND DATES	71
THE "EDUCATOR"	73
OVERSHARING	76
MY BORDERLINE PERSONALITY LATE NIGHT FRIEND	80
OUCH!	83
STAN THE NICE, TRIVIA GENIUS MAN:	85

TIME GOES BY	**86**
STRANGER THAN FICTION	**91**
TEENAGE CRUSH TIMES TWO	**95**
JONATHAN PART ONE	**99**
JONATHAN PART TWO	**108**
JONATHAN AND MOLLY… AND THE WORLD	**112**
THE TURNING POINT	**120**
TIME HEALS	**129**
LIFE GOES ON	**131**
A NEW HOME	**134**
ONE YEAR LATER	**136**

SIXTY IS THE NEW....21?!

Molly Bartlett here. This is my story, of seeing my life turned upside down at almost 60 years old, and finding a new beginning, using more strength than I knew I had. I'm not a cute 20 something, or a thirty something hottie, or even a forty something milf who created a new life after major illness or divorce. I am not a celebrity sharing their memoirs. I never had sex with a famous movie star, or even a soap opera actor.

Maybe I'm like you, a reasonably attractive, healthy 58-year-old mom and professional woman. I decided to write my story to hopefully inspire a woman or two who, like me, has reached the age of feeling "invisible", to let them know you can become visible again and feel totally alive, even after tragedy. (*And who doesn't encounter some of that along the road?)*

I told my adult kids I was doing this, and they were supportive, but asked me not to embarrass them too much. Isn't that a mother's job? I suggested they could be my editors if they wished. Robbie said he trusted Lizzie to do the editing job. She has put a thumbs down on some of my ideas, such as the first title I had thought of for this book.

"Getting my sexy back at 60". Her reaction was a resounding "That's soooo grooss." "NOOOOOOOOOOOO!" Finding a title for this book was going to take a little more time.

Why did I pick that title? That's sort of what happened to me, through no choice of my own. I was thrust back into the single world, forced to take a long hard look at who I was, just me, not me as a couple. I learned how to navigate in the real world and online. Tall order when your last date with someone other than your husband was in 1977, when there was no such thing as an internet. (Even Al Gore didn't mention the internet until 1999) So online dating was not anything I could have even imagined.

This new life has had its moments, funny, frustrating, icky, good, and bad. To give you a taste of what's to come allow me to introduce you to:

Peter the Pickle Man

A bit later in my story I will share my experience with learning the ins and outs of online dating. But let's start with one of the first men I went out with, a man I met on the internet. Peter is a finance guy, nice looking in a bland way, tall, slim, blonde-ish.

After a couple of days of texting Peter asked me to meet him for dinner. He worked in Manhattan, not far from my office. We met at a restaurant close to Grand Central. Our conversation was too boring to mention unless you have a real interest in investing in ETF's. I frankly just think of them mainly as letters of the alphabet. The night got more "interesting" when Peter's hamburger came. He casually reached into his pocket and took out his own four-inch-long dill pickle.

"You bring your own pickle to restaurants?? On dates?!!!"

I was amazed.

"The right dill pickle is key to the hamburger experience. "

I countered with: "I see it's a long one."

"The right size is 4 to 6 inches. "Peter informed me and then asked:

"Would you like to try my pickle?"

"No sorry, I never try a guy's pickle on a first date."

Peter the dry finance guy with a pickle obsession had no clue what I was talking about.

"You sure? I have one nice sized bite left."

"Positive. That's too much pickle for me"

I was also positive I would NEVER want to have a bite of Peter's pickle, or to see him again. I met a whole bunch of "Peters" with pretty amusing stories I will share with you later.

BACKSTORY

First, I should share how I got to this place in my life. This is the hard part of the story. It was 2015. My husband Marty's baby sister Linda, a highly respected estate and trust attorney, who at almost 50 years old was finally marrying her perfect mate.

Susan, a 55-year-old emergency room nurse, was the nurturing partner Linda had always wanted. Laugh out loud funny and smart, Susan also had a Broadway belter's singing voice and regaled us with show tunes at all family events. This was particularly attractive to me since I had always dreamed of a career in theater. Can't dance but I can sing and act a little. Marty and I had always made a good team that way, singing at family gatherings together, to the delight, and disgust of our kids, depending on their mood and their age.

Linda and Susan had put their combined brilliant minds together to plan the perfect wedding, with every detail meticulously considered.

Marty was psyched for the promised "spectacular food". My living large husband loved food and believed potato chips were a food group. And he never met an ice cream flavor he didn't adore. This had translated into needing two stents in his heart already. Under my watchful eye he had been on a low cholesterol diet for several years. I was waiting for Marty to be ready to go and was watching the clock impatiently.

"Marty, what are you doing up there? We're going to be late!"

"Almost ready…"

"Are you putting on MAKEUP?! "

It's just getting this kilt on…"

"Marty, no, you're not wearing the kilt! You outgrew that 15 years ago."

"I know…"

"What's the deal?"

"I bought another one."

Marty was very proud of his Irish heritage and loved getting dressed up in the kilt. He could also play the bagpipes. but not near as well as he thought he could.

I came into our bedroom and there he was admiring himself in our full-length mirror.

"Gorgeous! You're wearing underwear, right?"

"Yes, "

"Thank goodness for that."

"You're not really supposed to though."

"Glad you made an exception. And that NEW kilt seems a bit tight already."

"It's grand! I had to wear the kilt, Moll; Linda would be disappointed if I didn't."

"Not sure about that, your brother isn't gonna wear one!"

"He wasn't born in Ireland."

"Marty you were 12 months old when you came from the 'olde' country."

"It's in me bones me darling!"

At which point Marty waltzed me around the room singing "When Irish Eyes are Smiling".

We made it just in time for Marty to play the bagpipes as he had insisted to Linda he had to do, at the ceremony. The cocktail hour was everything they had promised. After

2 Margaritas I told Marty I would get food for both of us, hoping to edit out the danger foods from Marty's plate. Marty called after me... "Special occasions it's ok to break the diet Moll, Doctor Bob even agrees."

I was feeling pretty relaxed at this point, so I decided Marty was right. He deserved to enjoy in celebration of little sis's wedding. I treated him to a pile of his favorite chipotle chicken wings.

Marty smiled his huge, dimpled smile and winked at me when I came back to the table. "Miss Molly, you got through that line so fast, you're unsinkable! "Marty loved to use certain adoring phrases repeatedly and using my name together with the reference to "The Unsinkable Molly Brown" was one of his faves.

Marty and Linda's banker brother, Jerry poked me in the ribs with his usual swagger and over the top confidence and said "C'mon sista they're playing our song". So off to the dance floor we went.

A while later I looked over to our table and couldn't believe what I saw. Marty was on the floor, all 250 kilt wearing pounds of him, chicken bone lodged in his throat. Susan, the emergency room nurse/ bride ran over to perform CPR– the whole room froze. And my heart started to break...into a million little pieces.

Fast forward past the aborted reception. Marty didn't make it. The funeral was several days later, and at least he had a new suit. The one I had wanted him to wear to the wedding, now he wore it to his funeral.

I am not writing this book to tell the tragic story of how I lost the love of my life. It's really about what happened AFTER that. How at 58 years old, I managed to start over. But for context I'll share a bit more about Marty and me.

Marty had been my everything since I was 20 years old. We met "cute" at a frat party at Iona College, in New Rochelle, NY. I walked into the loud crowded room and saw this handsome dude across the room. Like a rom- com, except I tripped over the beer drenched carpet and fell headfirst into the lap of this adorable curly haired, Colin Farrell lookalike (only chubbier) with a great smile and killer wink. His frat boy buddies began laughing uproariously and Marty, who could never resist a good joke said… "I told ya the prettiest ones always fall head over heels for me" At which point I raced out of that stinky frat house.

Marty came sprinting after me, smiled and sincerely said, "Dumb joke, sorry, sorry, sorry…. you didn't deserve that. Wanna hear how I face planted in the macaroni salad bowl in the fraternity dining room yesterday?" I cracked up and that was the beginning.

Thirty-eight years later we had a Victorian style house in Sleepy Hollow, NY. It even has a white picket fence, which has needed to be fixed for years. Marty kept saying he would get to that and all his "visions" for the house soon. As a very successful general contractor you would think he would have, but that attention deficit disorder thing of his always got in the way.

We had our twins, Robbie, and Lizzie, who were 26 years old at that point, and our rescue basset hounds, Estelle and Sheila, who kept me busy cleaning up their drool all day long. I believed this would always be my life. We had a good, but of course not perfect marriage. Marty and I have always been an example of opposites attracting and somehow making it work despite our differences, with lots of love, and lots of ups and downs.

AFTER THE FUNERAL

Anyone who has ever lost a spouse knows the anguish of those first days and months, the feeling of being dropped into a dark endless pit that you think you will never crawl out of. The droves of friends and neighbors bringing you more casseroles than you've ever seen in your life. And then after the kids find their way back to their own lives, the people you barely know offering to take you out to dinner. I found this a little weird, because if we hadn't had dinner before, why would we enjoy each other's company now?

But all these well-meaning, if sometimes odd offerings of sympathy do help you start to slowly make your way forward. I am grateful for all the kindness. It did help.

Having a really good, and somewhat dark sense of humor doesn't hurt either. To amuse myself I started compiling a list of my favorite over the top sympathetic comments, to name just a few:

The dry cleaner who Marty had gone to for 15 years, when I told him that Marty had passed away said with great sadness,
"Are you sure?" *(And I'm thinking if he hasn't, we sure shouldn't have spent all that money on a funeral)*
The friend of a friend who said to me: "You should meet my friend" *(everybody has a friend you should meet)*. "My friend makes me think of you. Her husband has been gone for 5 years and she still says she will never be happy again and she would like someone to throw her in with him, in his funeral plot."

My response to this was to jump across the table *(Marty had been gone only 3 months at the time)* and to shout… "THAT WILL NOT BE ME!"

And of course, there were the people I knew vaguely who gave me those looooong, sad faces on the train and then turned to whisper to their travel companion, "THAT'S HER! YOU KNOW THE POOR DEAR WHOSE HUSBAND CHOKED ON A CHICKEN BONE."

All of this taught me one lesson, Marty might be gone, but I was very much still here. And I had no interest in being defined forever as the pathetic widow of Marty Bartlett. As he would have said, "Not gonna do it."

Everyone has their own way of getting through. My way included watching the most benign television shows possible: weird sports challenges, singing competitions, and absolutely nothing that has anything to do with happily married couples. After a month, I trudged back into my small office, at the tiny public relations agency I had founded, and tried to jump back into working life. The distraction was helpful. But what do you do in the off time? The weekends? The long nights. I tried accepting the invitations to getaways as the 5th wheel with other couples. That got old quick. These were the people that Marty and I had spent countless days and nights with, and there was a giant hole in the room when we all got together.

I thought a weekend away with Linda and Susan would be soothing, so I joined them at their weekend house in the Berkshires. The walks in the woods were lovely but provided way too much time to think. And watching them snuggle in newlywedded bliss only reminded me of what I had lost. As for the show tune sing-a-longs Susan did a great impression of Barbara Streisand's "Don't rain on my parade." But that just reminded me that my parade had just been hit with a devastating hurricane.

After about 11 months of this I think the last straw was sitting in the back seat of my friend's car, like I was their 10-year-old child, on the way to a wedding, 4 hours from home. I had the distinct pleasure of listening to Janet and Ted have one of their spats over directions, Janet said "Gee you get to ride up to the wedding and see inside our marriage, and you get to ride home with Patty and Phil and get an inside view of theirs." I smiled, nodded, and said, "That's why I'm seriously considering joining match.com when we get home."

I had to find a way to make my own next chapter, much as I hated that phrase. I had always thought Marty would be the whole book.

It was nice that friends were willing to include a seat at their tables for me, and even a spare bedroom if I needed it. That was comforting, particularly at first, when I couldn't bear the thought of a future without Marty in it. But I was beginning to realize I needed to start putting energy into creating a new future.

BABY STEPS

I had to come to terms with the fact that being a WIDOW meant that I was also SINGLE. That might seem obvious, but somehow it wasn't. I had not been single, without a boyfriend, fiancé, or spouse since I was 20 years old. I needed to understand being single was not something to fear. That was a tall order at my age. I don't think I had ever figured out how to be comfortable standing on my own, just me, and being good with it. I tried telling myself this would be an opportunity for growth.

And when it came to meeting men, what could I do? I am not a "hang at the bar girl kind of girl". I had been curious about this online dating thing. Now I was really considering it as an option. First step, I looked at what was out there, as a "newborn" single in 2015. It was eye opening, dating sites for dog lovers, Italian people, Jewish people, sites for women to make the first move, for older singles and of course, match.com. There was also a site with the weird name of Zoosk. In my techno stupidity while shopping around on these sites I somehow managed to sign up for several of them at once, by accident. This led to my inbox flooded with dog lovers, Italian men, Jewish men, older men, whoa. It took me a little time to untangle all that. I wasn't even ready to join one site never mind 5!

On top of that, I was overwhelmed by a sudden change in the way men were looking at me. Not necessarily men I would be interested in, but still, it was surprising. The divorced electrician was lingering and repeatedly explaining the house's ancient wiring to me. The beverage cart guy in Grand Central was telling me jokes like Henny

Youngman, and a thirty something year old waiter with a thick *(and adorable)* Italian accent passed me his number when he brought me my cappuccino. NONE of these things had happened to me in years. Was I wearing a flashing neon sign that said "Available, available!" Or was I checking out men in a way I hadn't before?

Online dating may be second nature for twenty and thirty somethings, but for someone who hadn't been on a date in over 30 years??? I started out reading profiles and looking at pictures of women who would be "my competition" and men. Looking at the women's profiles I quickly decided I would not be modeling myself after a lot of the women I saw. 50 somethings in string bikinis?! Or women with flirtatious profiles that made me blush. That was the last time I looked at other womens' profiles. I would just be me and not worry about what others do. In checking out the men's' profiles, I was fascinated by how many included pictures of themselves holding giant fish or posing next to the biggest motorcycles I had ever seen. I got the symbolism – ugh.

As for what they had to say about themselves some guys wanted to ride up on a white horse, grab a woman, dressed in a billowing white dress, and gallop down the beach into the sunset. I was sure if that happened to me my dress would get stuck under my shoe, and I would fall off the horse. What real guy says these things anyway?! Others at least just said: enjoy jogging, watching the Knicks and going out for a good pizza. Boring, but believable.

I was far from ready to find a new handsome prince, but I figured by the time I was, maybe I would have a better handle on this dating thing. And it would give me something to do to occupy the long nights ahead. The twins had their own apartment they shared in White Plains, which meant my only company was Estelle and Sheila. While a good snuggle with a drooly basset hound is lovely, I missed the hugs, the spooning, the human contact. The nights dragged on endlessly, and the silence was deafening.

I decided I would take the giant step of creating a profile with pictures. I found a picture my kids had taken of me with Estelle and Sheila. Who wouldn't be tantalized by those adorable basset faces?

DARBY'S WORLD

I came into work on a Monday morning and talked to my office manager and "being single cheerleader, Darby" about my thoughts on entering the world of dating. I knew Darby would be helpful. Darby came into our lives a dozen years ago when her husband went out to get a newspaper and never came back. Not kidding, it really happened to her. To restart her life, she started going to a local social club in NY and met Joe, one of the guys who worked for Marty. Darby needed a new job and recognizing her intelligence, Joe introduced her to Marty. She became Marty's treasured office manager for several years.

Darby is the most unique human I have ever known. Not even 5 feet tall, 85 pounds, with bright, shiny pink shoulder length hair that she meticulously colors each month, she looks like some sort of magical creature invented by J.K Rowling. Darby dresses all in black, with these giant black work boots that look way too big for her tiny body. Her clothes look worn, except for the colorful scarves, all with some sort of pink pattern, that she sometimes highlights her look with. Darby has a thick cockney accent that makes it tough to understand what she is saying at times, but once you get the gist of it there is generally some real- life wisdom amid her colorful speech and surprisingly bawdy humor.

After I had known Darby for a couple of years, she shared her unique life story with me. Darby was born into a Hasidic Jewish family and her early years are a bit vague. Not sure if she was born in Turkey, or in Israel. Her father is a brilliant architect and a rabbinical scholar. His knowledge took him to building sites all over the world. Darby and her two younger siblings were along for the ride. Darby's mind is like a sponge and her many travels led her to become fluent in multiple languages: English, Spanish, French, Hebrew, Yiddish, and several African dialects.

Darby's mother had run away when Darby was just a little girl, without telling anyone why, or where she was going. The rigid constraints put upon women in the Hasidic culture must have been too much for this spirited woman. It seemed to me Darby must have inherited her spunk from her mom. Darby's appetite for adventure and enjoying life is 3 times larger than her tiny size. And when she comes whirling into a room it's like pink fairy dust surrounds her.

Darby helped her father raise her younger sister and brother and once they were teenagers, she could no longer bear the rigidity of the Hasidic world either. She was too curious, too smart, and too free spirited.

Over the course of time, she would announce more pieces of her story. Over dinner one night she mentioned to Lizzie and me that Qaddafi did have his good sides. I said "What?! Omar Qaddafi! He was a monster!" She said "Yah, but he was good to Afrique in some ways. Me papa did some work for him, we lived in Libya for a bit."
"How did that work, your Jewish!"
"Right, he didn't know that. We disguised ourselves. He would have killed us for sure."
She stated these things in such a calm "Mary Poppins-esque" spit spot way that we were left not knowing what to

say. And this was just one of many outrageous things she would share about her past.

Looking at a map one day after this I was struck by how she may have ended up having such a love for Africa. Her dad's work travels took her down from Libya into Africa. She was able to see for herself the way the Islamic culture was affecting the children of Africa. The constraints on education for all, but especially the young girls, the prevalence of female genital mutilation, the constant fear of terrorism and the desperate need for improved nutrition and clean water.

While Darby had the benefits of education and a much better standard of living, she could relate to the feeling of being oppressed by your own culture. She was drawn to the people of Africa as a calling, to help. After her heart was broken by an American man while trying to live as an American professional and artist, she began to think how she could find more meaning in her life. She found that meaning in West Africa.

One might think that many of her stories were total invention, but during her many long stays in "Afrique" as she called it, she sent me pictures and videos of her with her buddies in the local villages, and also pictures of her as she worked alongside them mining for gold, and teaching classes at the local school. I have had many FaceTime conversations with them all.

The children who she lovingly called "my kids", these children took the place in her heart for the child she had always wanted but as a woman in her forties now, she was coming to terms with the fact that a child of her own would probably never happen. She poured most of the money she made prospecting for gold in Mali back into helping the children of her adopted country, buying books, food and whatever they needed.

Darby had created a lifestyle all her own, spending months in Africa and then months back in the US. She would rent out her apartment to West African immigrants who were getting their footing in America while she was gone, helping them and herself. When she was back, she would work for us and then spend several nights a week teaching English at one of the African consulates. She had so ingratiated herself to Marty and to me that we made this unique situation work.

Then Darby disappeared from our lives for a full year on one of these trips to Africa. Marty couldn't keep her job open for that long, and that's how she came to be working for me when she returned. She has been a blessing. A brilliant bookkeeper, a fabulous phone salesperson, and loaded with creative ideas that helped us land new accounts. Some people find her unconventional looks and colorful language are a bit much. I was constantly gently requesting that she tone it down at the office. She toned it down…. a teeny tiny bit.

When I told Darby, I thought I was ready to stick a toe into the dating waters she was thrilled. "Ah me lady yis must do this!
 Ye know Marty would celebrate it n tell u to keep going with the passion yis have for livin n lovin."
 "I don't think a lot of people in my life will approve"

"Me darling we are here to live with an inexplicable forceful lust n passion for life, for having been alive each day in the first place! Anyone who knows u should believe u must do this!"

Darby has this belief we were sisters in another life, and I think this might be true. Ridiculous? Me this middle of the road Jewish girl born in Brooklyn; NY, who looks like what Katie Couric would look like if she happened to have middle European parent? Pretty in a perky cheerleader way. But it was the essence of us that formed the glue, a core honesty, humor, and enthusiasm for life.

Darby couldn't wait to look at men's profiles with me, it was like holding back a wild stallion. She agreed to wait on this when I said maybe we should start with my profile. I showed her the picture of me with Sheila and Estelle for my profile and she was kind as always, but she had other ideas, and told me she would be coming to my place for a photo shoot over the weekend.

Darby's photo shoot was way more entertaining than my own had been. First, she grabbed my old guitar from the closet and said I should pose with it.
"This will be brilliant me darling."
"But Darby I haven't played this thing in 15 years."
"No matter me soul sister, this will be brill."
"Ok…."
It turned out to be a great picture, but hopefully no man will ask me to play that guitar. I can only play "So Far Away" the Carole King song. And when I used to play it, Marty and his college buddies used to beg me to play it "so far away".

Next Darby decided we needed to make me look a bit more "adventurous". I suggested I climb a tree in the backyard. We tried that out and Darby was underwhelmed. She had another idea… "Come me lady" (I always feel like British royalty when she calls me "me lady".) Darby squinted up at me balanced on a tree limb and said:

"Ye look like you're about to fall."

"Makes sense I feel like I'm going to fall. Did I say I was good at climbing trees?!"

Darby sighed, took the picture, and then took me into our big, beautiful hall bathroom, one of Marty's projects that he finished.

My photo shoot director Darby directed me to sit on the counter of the sink. I protested. "Darby this is weird."

"Weird is good. You'll stand out."

It turned out to be an oddly flattering picture, and Darby said it showed off "me guns".

I now had a couple of "decent pictures" according to Darby, and I needed a profile name. I suggested Molly, lol. Darby rejected that. Looking around the kitchen and talking to herself Darby opened the freezer and saw a Sara Lee cheesecake and exclaimed "Perfection! Sara Lee, like the luscious lady yis are."

I rolled my eyes but once Darby is rolling you gotta get out of the way of the train, or you'll be flattened.

Now with a name that suggested luscious baked goods, and a super picture of me sitting on the bathroom counter, all I needed to do was write my profile and I would be ready to give this online dating thing a trial run!

Darby said, "Wait you are not ready to write that profile."
Now I was confused.
"I thought you were super excited about this online dating thing for me…"
"Me lady you need to have some fun first, we need to see a new Molly."
I was a bit put off, but willing to listen.
"Monday after work we are goin out me lady."
And Monday was the first of my "learning how to float as a single person" lessons with Darby.

Darby took me to the Metropolitan Museum of Art. That seemed like an odd choice for me to start thinking like a young single lady. But a trip to anywhere with Darby can get you back into the spirit of living. It quickly became apparent that Darby had practically memorized every exhibit in the museum and loved every bit of it. We walked in and Darby immediately grabbed my hand and sprinted to the closest exhibit. A gigantic smile on her face and a well of tears in her eyes she started explaining why this one piece of art was so meaningful to her. Then she moved on to the next, and then the next, and the next. Darby continued to pull me into the wonder and awe she felt here for two solid hours.

Darby's ability to see the beauty in life everywhere is contagious and I could feel my sad soul starting to awaken again just the tiniest bit. Marty had never been thrilled with museum trips and I had forgotten how much I enjoyed them. This was Darby day trip one, others would follow. Each Darby outing would be a gift to my soul, and a little push to finding out who I was on my own.

ROBBIE AND LIZZIE

Darby had always been close to our whole family and loved the twins. She worried about how they would move forward, and I did too. Robbie is the light-hearted athlete with a twinkle in his eye, a lot like his dad. Robbie works as a fifth-grade social studies teacher and lacrosse coach. He talks about law school some day in the future, but for now he is enjoying life. He misses his dad terribly but his friends and the kids who adore Coach Rob are a huge help.

Lizzie is the one that concerns me, and Darby. Lizzie has always been quiet and studious. Her Dad tried to get her into sports. He coached a softball team and Lizzie would happily sit in the outfield picking daisies. Ultimately, he gave up. Lizzie loved to spend her time playing the violin. Where she got this intense love of the violin, who knows? Marty's mom sang vaudeville on Broadway, and Marty and I love music and love to sing, but that is as close as I could get to figuring out her musical instrument talent. Her violin skills took her to college on a scholarship and now she is employed playing in the orchestra for "Phantom of the Opera".

I know Lizzie found our family game nights childish. And I often thought she felt like a stranger in a strange land with Marty, Robbie, and me. That said, she worshipped her dad, and he treated her with the respect and love she deserved. She happened to be between boyfriends when her dad passed away. A lonely time, but I was glad she and her brother had each other as company in their shared apartment.

Darby believed that Lizzie could do with some "lightening up" and would invite her along on some of our evening outings when Lizzie had a night off from playing in the orchestra. One night happened to be during "Sailors' Week" in Manhattan. The 3 of us went to dinner at a restaurant with music in mid-town. Darby went outside to smoke one of her many cigarettes. When she came back, she brought 3 new friends with her, 3 young sailors, in their starched white sailor uniforms, who she had instantly befriended on the street. The boys sat down with us, and it was more fun than I've had in a long time, with Darby and the sailors trading stories about their adventures around the world. All of us got up and danced. *(No, it wasn't a dance club, but that didn't stop us)* One of the boys asked for Lizzie's number, not sure if she gave him a real one, but I do know she had fun that night. Darby was teaching us how to laugh again.

Wherever we went with Darby we would meet new people, whether they were sitting at the next table, speaking an African dialect, and she would strike up a conversation about her time in Sierra Leone, or Mali, or finding out the waitress used to live in the same neighborhood in London that she did in her teen years.

Walking down the street we would encounter friends she had made everywhere we would go. She would hug the coffee truck man and ask about his family while he handed her a free coffee. It was eye opening, and it helped Lizzie and me realize there was still joy in life, even if Marty wasn't here to be part of it.

THE MAKEOVER

Now that I had begrudgingly accepted my single woman status, it occurred to me I needed to make some changes in jewelry and wardrobe. Riding into the city after a year of widowhood, I looked down at the rings on my hands and realized it was time to stop wearing my engagement ring and wedding band. Step one, I put them on a thin gold necklace that I hid underneath my shirt. Darby said nothing for a week or two, then commented:

"Me lady, Marty would tell u to ditch the gold prison."

"What do you mean?"

"It's time to not be goin steady and leave that chain in your bedroom."

I sighed and after another day or two I put the rings away in my home safe. I cried so much my eyes looked like I had developed a pink eye disease. I am trying to make this as upbeat as possible, but pain is part of it. I had plenty. The weddings where the bandleader said "Now it's time to get up and dance with that special someone" and for me it was time to run straight for the exit and hide in the stairwell. The incredible silence of every night. The quiet screamed at me in every room of the house. I spent practically every night sitting in one spot on the couch in the living room. Now it's permanently indented. After watching my mindless television shows I would go straight to my one spot in my bed, exactly where I would sleep when I shared the bed with Marty, not considering I could spread out a little more now. Spreading out and in the bed, living in the whole house would have been to admit Marty was gone. Marty's bathrobe remained hanging on the bathroom door. His shirts that needed to be dry-cleaned stayed in the hamper for months. Every now and then I would open the hamper and take out a shirt and take a whiff, to breathe in the scent of Marty.

Then there is the anger. I have always been an easy to get along with person, right up until… I'm not. My fuse is long but in those first months that fuse could ignite way easier and sometimes irrationally. For instance, in my frustration at returning some clothing I had bought at a store before Marty had died, the manager was not at all sympathetic to why it had taken me 7 months to return the items. I started screaming at her about "Widows should be treated with more sensitivity." I flounced out of that store and immediately backed my car into another one in the parking lot.

In those first agonizing days, weeks, and months after Marty's passing it was all about putting one foot in front of the other, to keep walking, I would even say this to myself as I drove to the train station, got on the train, and pushed myself to go into my office. I vowed to keep a sense of humor to protect my sanity and my kids, and to convince other people I wouldn't be a bummer to hang out with.

Bit by bit it got a little easier to make it through the day. At first the kids would take turns staying over-night, "mommy sitting", but after a few months I wanted them to stop. I wanted them to move forward themselves. That's when the quiet of the nights hit me hardest. And I had to face the fact that Marty wasn't coming back, and I did not want to not spend my life alone.

About six months after Marty died my wise and wonderful financial advisor/friend, Steve sat me down to do one of his financial goals exercises. Steve was really part therapist and part financial advisor. He believed his job was to help clients realize their life goals, as money related to it, and he was good at it. Steve asked me what my goals for the future were, not just financial but personal as well. My gut response without thinking was "to find love again".

I consider myself an evolved woman. I am proud of what I can achieve standing on my own two feet. But I did want love, and I don't think that made me less of an enlightened soul. After all, if love wasn't so important to so many people there wouldn't be so many chart- topping songs written about finding love, losing love, keeping love….

Over time I would evolve that thinking to four simple words – love, laughter, friendship, purpose – (a slogan lol – I am a public relations writer after all) Finding and nurturing these 4 things was my goal as the new, single Molly Bartlett.

I have always been goal oriented. Once I see the goal I will be in relentless pursuit, and I generally achieve it. This is part OCD related, and partially because I have never been "the best" at anything. I have always had to work twice as hard as my "over- achieving" classmates and work colleagues. At the end of the day, not being "the best" at anything may have been a positive, because my hard work often pays off. I decided to focus on the "finding love" part of my mantra first. Now that Marty was no longer here to love me, I was determined to find someone who I could love and who would love me back. I knew it would be different, but I was open to different.

I knew I had to take those first steps, to put away the rings. That alone was a huge undertaking. Then I had to start thinking about what did I want? I had spent so many years making decisions based on what was good for…Marty, deciding on groceries according to Marty's favorite meals. Restaurants based on Marty's picky eating habits. TV shows based on avoiding Marty making snarky remarks about my love of watching American Idol, and even choosing friends based on which ones Marty like. All of this was so second nature to me that I did not know what my opinion was, just mine, and what was my opinion as Marty's wife.

Then there was clothing. Marty loved a "vineyard vines" vibe. I secretly wasn't too crazy about it, but he was so complimentary when I dressed in a preppy girl way that I went along with it. Secretly I dreamed of looking like an Italian vogue model, even though I'm way too short for it, or just a little sexier. Now I was ready to find a new Molly way of dressing. New hairdo? Who knows.

I enlisted the help of Darby and my French journalist friend Claudine. This may not have been my wisest choice. Two totally different points of view are almost impossible to find. Darby was all for a look I would call "suburban hooker Mom".

"Me lady you have to get your sexy back" Darby would say, while doing some ludicrous "sexy" moves.

Claudine was all about long flowing high fashion tops that didn't work so well with my short curvy body, but looked amazing on her slim, straight 5' 10' frame. Taking them both shopping with me was interesting. Both speak fluent French, and they had discussions, just short of heated, about how they pictured the "new Molly" looking. From what I could make out based on my high school French class knowledge, Darby was convinced I needed to be more "uninhibited in my look." Claudine was sure Darby's choices might get me attention, but NOT from the right audience. Claudine thought her choices would make me look high class. Darby said something to the effect of they made me look like a sexless librarian.

After politely purchasing several of each of their selections we did something more useful. We went to dinner and drinks and had fun. The next day I returned all the clothes. This "new Molly" still had to look like the essence of "old Molly". I took myself to the local Lord & Taylor's and found some new tops in black, then some fabulous bright colors, including a new style at the time, cold shoulder, cashmere electric blue top, and jeans that weren't Momma jeans, one pair of 7's, one pair of Hudsons. I also treated myself to a pair of gorgeous and expensive boots and a luxurious leather jacket. This would be "the new Molly". No more Vineyard Vines. I felt good about my choices. Then I stopped at the Bobbie Brown makeup counter and bought new makeup from a great looking young woman who complimented my "beautiful skin" so effusively that I spent a small fortune.

Finally, there was the hair. I've never been adventurous with my hair styles, and now I took a baby step, adding low lights, highlights, just enough to make me look like a zebra. This sent me back to the salon the next day for a corrective color session. It was trial and error, but progress was being made.

GUILTY FEELINGS

Up until my first steps toward a "Molly makeover" I had been under the constant watchful eyes of a group I will affectionately call "the Mom Squad". Some of these women had been my friends since high school, we had all come back to raise our kids in the same area where we grew up. And we had banded together from baby play groups to carpooling and beyond, had girls' nights and girls' weekends away, family nights, rescued each other's lost cats, dogs, even ferrets, and hamsters. We discussed horrible homework assignments and frustrating husband situations. We knew each other so well, and best of all we knew how to enjoy a good laugh together, sometimes at each other's expense, but it was all coming from love and familiarity. We were there for each other 1000%.

When Marty passed away, they were as devoted to me as a pack of St. Bernhards. They saved me during those early days and months, keeping me fed, inviting me over on the lonely nights, helping me finally take his dirty dress shirts out of the hamper. I admit they had to tear those out of my hands, his bathrobe off the hook on the bathroom door and to move his clothes out of his closet. I will be forever grateful to this devoted team.

The hard part for us all was now I was in a different place in my life than all of them. I needed to chart my own course. This was a difficult concept for everyone to understand. They wanted to protect me from falling, just like you do with your kids when they are learning to walk. But a toddler needs to fall and bang into a few walls, so they can figure out how to stand up on their own, and so did I. I instinctively knew this, and when I first started thinking about trying online dating, I decided to keep it to myself until I felt more confident, and less guilty.

I couldn't shake the feeling that I was cheating on Marty. I kept reminding myself of his jokes about someday, after he was gone, he wanted me to have an outrageous affair with that romance novel cover model, Fabio. Marty would want me to have a life, and I also knew ultimately my friends and family would too, but what my head knew wasn't necessarily what my heart could understand.

I also felt I was somehow responsible for his death. The autopsy revealed he had a heart attack, not surprising based on his lifestyle choices. That made me even angrier at myself for giving in to his food cravings! Even if the chicken bones hadn't killed him, I could somehow have protected him if I had watched over him better. I spent many nights torturing myself about my culpability in his death. So, I continued to keep my future thinking to myself, except for Claudine and Darby, and thanks to Darby, Joe the medium.

SPIRITUAL HELP

I have never been a religious person but as I have grown older, I have become "spiritual". I believe we go on, not sure how, but I think it's kind of like the internet. We are all made of electricity and somehow that goes on. I have had so many experiences that have led me to believe in some sort of afterlife. When Marty was alive the lamp in our bedroom would turn itself on around midnight generally on holidays related to my dad – my dad's birthday or Father's Day. Marty was pretty sure it was my dad checking to see everything was ok, but Marty said:

"Hal should get the hell out of our bedroom."

I had many strange, unexplainable experiences. Songs would start playing on relevant days to dead family members on my iPhone, out of the blue. Songs that were favorites of the person who had passed. Like the day I walked out of my mom's house as she lay on her death bed. She had hospice there and it was to be the last time I would see her. My iPhone suddenly started playing a Mariah Carey song I had never listened to that was in my library. "Never forget you." These experiences made me curious about visiting a medium. But I wanted someone I was convinced was credible, not one of those storefront types that say "tarot card readings" with a lady dressed like a gypsy.

Darby told me about Joe. She had gone to see him after she learned her mom died. Darby hadn't seen her mom since she was a little girl. After her mom had left the family, she had restarted her life in Israel. Darby wanted to ask her why she had left them. She did her homework and found Joe. Darby kept telling me about her experiences connecting with her mom through Joe. She kept encouraging me to call him. I was intrigued. Joe has written books; he's been all over the air waves. I made my first appointment.

I drove up to Joe's normal looking house in Ridgefield, CT (Not sure what I was expecting, maybe a house like in The Munster's tv show?) When greeted by Joe I was surprised at his physical presence. Far from looking like some gypsy with tarot cards, Joe looked like he could have been my financial advisor, tall, handsome, and well spoken. Joe had been in finance and had his psychology degree.

The first thing he said to me after I sat down was, "I see a man here who looks a little like some Irish actor, what's that guy's name… Colin Farrell… only chubbier.
He's telling me that his passing was dramatic, right?"
"Yea it was"
"Why does he keep talking about sauce and chicken bones?"
"He was eating chicken wings…"
"And I GAVE THEM TO HIM – I FEEL LIKE A MURDERER."
"Wait, he's saying hold on"
"You didn't…"
"Yes, I did…"
"No, he says he got more"
"He did?"
"Yea, he says stop torturing yourself, you left the table"
Right, I was dancing, for a while, too long."
"He went and got more…and anyway"
– it wasn't really the chicken wings "

"He was in bad shape"

"He said something about his heart…he wants you to get on with your life"

"I'm trying"

"He says try harder. "

"And what's with all the blankets all over the couches?

"For Sheila and Estelle, my dogs, they make a mess."

"But so many blankets? "

"They make a BIG mess."

"He says YOU should get out from under "the blankets" and start living."

"That's what his sister and brother say…"

"Listen to them."

He says they really love you.

They are there for you."

"I know, I know, but I feel guilty about moving on, I can't picture telling them."

"They want you to, they will support you."

"My brother-in-law did help me throw out that 7-foot-tall plant of Marty's that was taking up half the den. It was half dead, and he said - c'mon let's get this out of here.

I said: But it was Marty's.

And he said, Honey, he's not here."

Joe said, take his advice. "Now it's time for you to get moving forward."

That first visit to Joe, and I have had a few since, helped me get past my initial guilt about starting a new life with less Martyness and more Molly.

GETTING OUT THERE

On one of the many nights when it was just Sheila, Estelle and me, and Jimmy Kimmel on the TV, I decided I had put in the time and effort towards my Molly makeover, I had received reassurance about letting go of my guilt from Joe, so maybe I should try creating that profile again. Or at least register with one of the online dating services. Registering meant answering a lot of annoying questions.

Was I going to be graded on this?

Would the wrong answers send me all the loser guys?

"What's my idea of a perfect afternoon?"

"What's the most romantic thing you can think of?"

UGH! I almost shut the computer...

but I figured meeting men this way beat going out to a bar.

Darby did drag me to one "singles type bar" one night. I couldn't believe all the 50 something ladies with cleavage spilling out of their too small bodycon dresses (how did they breathe?), downing cosmos and giggling over some dudes sitting across the bar. When it occurred to me, I was single just like them I felt a little vomit come up into my mouth and vowed I would NOT be single in that way.

That one night with Darby I downed a couple of glasses of wine and joined her in showing off our "dance moves", on top of the bar. Amazing I didn't fall off; my dance moves and my balancing abilities are not what I would call exemplary. Fun, but NOT how I wanted to meet a man.

So here I was once more, in the comfort of my home, answering questions that made me feel like I was 13 reading Tiger Beat magazine. You would think the basic questions would be easy. But no. Not even age. Claudine had insisted I make myself 5 years younger on the sites, because everybody makes themselves 5 years younger. I've never been a good liar, so while I stared at the computer and at this little ball you could spin to find your age, I accidentally spun it and it landed on 58. At this point I was 59. I could not change it. I couldn't figure out how. It was stuck on 58. It is NOT worth lying by a year, that would just confuse me. What year was I born again? Who played in the World Series that year? When would I be eligible for Social Security? One year was not worth the subterfuge that would go with it. Now I was stuck being Sara Lee, 58 years old, instead of Molly 59.

After this I was back to creating that profile. Thanks to Darby's adventures with me pre-profile writing, I managed to laugh my way through this with more ease I made it short and sweet, and marginally flirtatious. I attached my bathroom counter picture, the guitar playing picture, and I added the one with Sheila, Estelle, and me. I liked that one, even if I had been told it was not a good idea to use it.

I flipped through the faces of men on the site. OMG the faces! Why would anyone think some of these shots were attractive? Men in old overalls, with missing teeth. Unsmiling faces in ugly suits that made them look like used car salesmen. So many looong profiles. So many men who were in touch with their feminine side. I was having trouble believing it. The responses I started to receive on my profile were…interesting.

"Hey baby what song are you going to play on that guitar for me?"

Another said, "Sitting on the bathroom counter could be a good way for us to get up close and personal, know what I mean?"

One told me he was allergic to dogs, particularly hated dogs with big jowls that drool all over you. Sheila and Estelle don't enjoy men like you either buddy!

I kept reminding myself, even though it was scary that "Sara Lee" had been launched into cyberspace, I was safe in my own home. I was determined to approach this as an anthropological study or interactive video game. I vowed not to take any rejections too personally. I was ready to find the humor in anything, even if it was insulting, lewd or just plain stupid.

I set off on an educational trip into the world of online dating. I learned how to fight back against the algorithm to find people I wouldn't meet if it was left to artificial intelligence. I learned how to use google to keep myself safe. I also figured out how to spot scammers and bullshit artists. But online dating wasn't my whole world…

THE REAL WORLD GUY

Every day I woke up to my new reality. A day at the office. A night out with one of the Mom Squad, or to an event with some of my couple friends, which often made me feel sad and missing Marty even more than if I stayed home. Dinner with Robbie and Lizzie, or with Darby or Claudine. Or just me and my two dogs. The loneliness kept growing. In fact, so much so that I started thinking a recently divorced friend of a friend might be "the one". He was attractive. We knew the same people, had kids who shared the same friends. It would be "so perfect, such an easy fit". I decided I was a contemporary woman and could call him and ask him out.

"Hey George, it's Molly."
"Hey there Molly, you need help fixing that leaky faucet again?"
"Nope you fixed it perfectly. Better than ever."
"I was a plumber in a past life"
"I was actually thinking more about asking you to join me for dinner than for more plumbing help."
"Cool"

And that was the start of my first "fantasy life." This one entitled "Sundays in the park with George" like that Broadway show. I spent some Sundays taking walks in the park with George for real. There were also dinners out, bike rides, and lots of conversations about our kids, our mutual friends, our jobs. I was convincing myself maybe it could be this easy, I could move on right in the neighborhood. I'd just slot him in there. I was already imagining how much fun we would have with our mutual crew of friends. Life would go on, practically seamlessly, except for the giant hole in my heart where Marty was. Oh, and of course George had to go along with this little plan.

This was not the first plan I had to help me through the loneliness of having this old house that used to be filled with laughter and love. I had thought about renting out our finished basement for very little money to abused women so they would have another option other than going to a non-profit shelter. Robbie and Lizzie persuaded me this was probably not the best idea I had ever had. Then there was my vision of turning my basement into a cat sanctuary, helping the local humane society by taking in cats when they were overcrowded. I got as far as planning out how to rebuild the basement with roomy cages and open play areas when Lizzie reminded me that Sheila and Estelle are not wild about cats.

On the one hand I did realize that before I started to take this dating thing seriously, I still had to get more comfortable with me. What will give me gratification? What do I enjoy doing all on my own? Kind of like when the kids were little, and I worked so hard to teach them they could play by themselves and enjoy it. But then on the other hand, I was lonely. It's not like I hadn't travelled alone. I've been all over the country for my PR job. But in my personal life I had trouble seeing myself as independent. I had never broken away from being Shirley's daughter. And Shirley believed a woman without a spouse was bupkas. Translation from Yiddish – "absolutely nothing"

I had been fighting my mother's vision of a woman's value my whole life. I had a successful career, hobbies and volunteer work, as well as a husband and children. But to Shirley I could have been President of the United States, but the only thing that was important was having a husband and kids. So, without the husband I was now officially "bupkas".

Shirley passed away over six years ago, and my dad, Hal, has been gone a decade longer. Didn't matter, I could still hear Shirley in my ear judging everything I do. And I knew Shirley would have approved of George, a lawyer! I would have conversations with her in my head. "Mom he's attractive, but kind of old, social security age."

"But darling he still has all his hair and he's so nice and slim."

"Is that a crack about Marty?" Marty had lost a nice big round area on the top of his head, yamika style, which was the closest thing to anything Jewish about Marty. And he was no one's idea of slim.

George was in good shape due to his obsession with playing soccer, which had only grown more intense after his wife Joyce divorced him and ran off with someone, she met on one of her business trips. Joyce was now remarried and living in Las Vegas. Oh, I almost forgot, George had one other thing my mother admired, he had been a past president of the local conservative temple, the perfect man!

All of this is background to say I spent a lot of time fantasizing about how "perfect" a life with George could be. George and I had some nice times together including dinners out in Manhattan and Tarrytown. Our mutual acquaintances gave us a lot to laugh about. He knew my kids, I knew his youngest son, who is a year older than my kids (George has another son a couple of years older than that) How perfect right? Maybe not so much.

I should have started realizing we weren't right for each other when he told me he wasn't a fan of dogs and cats, particularly dogs who drool. Still, I was undeterred. After all he made me laugh, or wait, were we laughing because I kept cracking jokes? We talked about our losses, so similar on some levels and yet so different. Joyce was very much alive, even if she wasn't living any place nearby. George still hadn't gotten over it. He would ask me over and over…

"What didn't she get from me? I was home every night. We had great midnight talks.

And all she kept saying was she needed more. More what?"

"I know George it's so sad, you're so kind…"

Then there was that first kiss. George could kiss! What a talent! And if I hadn't been smitten already that would have done the trick.

Then there were the kisses after that. Never mind that George would send me playful texts and seem totally into me,

and then would disappear for days, even a week or two at a time. At this point I was a "teenaged Molly" again. All I could see was George and I had chemistry and a lot of friends in common, it didn't occur to me that a future is made of more than that. George was way ahead of me because he had 5 years of nursing his wounds, while I had only been a widow for a year. He would say wise things to me like:

"Get out there and go on some dates." I would say.
"That wouldn't make you jealous?"
He would say. "No, I think you need to do that."
I would tell him… "Wait that's not what you're supposed to say, tell me you'd be destroyed by it."
To this he would say "You crack me up."

So, visions of a future with George kept me busy for a few months. I saw him one, sometimes two nights a week. And except for the giant wall he put up on a regular basis, we had fun. We came close to taking that next step to an overnight date, but George always stopped himself. I was raring to go, *(Lizzie, "my editor" told me this was too much information for her – so I'll leave any more details of this out)*

I was one confused lady, scared of making love with anyone but Marty, yet ready to open that new page. I think George knew if we did there would be no turning back, our worlds were too closely connected, it couldn't be casual. I made a million excuses for it in my head and avoided the main one, George was not looking to have a future with me. Darby gave me plenty of excuses for why it wasn't happening.

"Poor Georgie he lives in awe of you me lady.
He's afraid he won't be good enough for ye."
I was very happy to believe her well intentioned reasoning. But then the day came that George told me he was moving to St. Croix.

"St. Croix, you're moving to a housing development called St. Croix?"

"No, the island."

"Why?"

"I need a totally new start."

"Wait I thought we were a new start."

"Moll, we can't be a new start, we knew each other's spouses way too well."

"So?"

"I can't just live in this same setting and take over Marty's shoes, I was friends with Marty, and you and Joyce were kind of friendly too.

It won't work for either of us"

"I thought it could…"

"You're still figuring things out, I like you and I am attracted to you, but the timing, the history, it can't work."

George sailed out of my life, and eventually into the arms of an "Island girl" in St. Croix. His best friend in Tarrytown told me he had thrown himself into learning scuba diving and his whole world was now based upon teaching scuba to tourists.

Good for him. Eventually I would realize how much we had helped each other blossom into new versions of ourselves, but in the beginning I just felt dissed.

His constant comments about my beauty and wisdom did help me believe I had a chance at finding new love, but I couldn't just snap my fingers and wish myself out of the loneliness. It wasn't going to happen by taking in boarders or setting up a cat sanctuary or by slotting an old friend into Marty's shoes. I was going to have to put my energy and inner strength into walking forward and reinventing my life.

INTERNET FIRSTS: FROM MR. KINKY SENSE OF HUMOR TO MR. WEEBLE.

After a few weeks of feeling sorry for myself I turned on the computer at 11 pm and went onto the Match website, checking out the faces that came up in front of me. There were a few that stunned me enough to say: "Oh my God if these are the options out there, kill me now."

I looked at my profile and decided I would take the picture of me with my two loyal basset hounds down. I rewrote my bio piece to make it shorter, wittier, less serious and pressed save. I closed the computer and went to bed. I would sit back down at the computer tomorrow night and see if my updated profile helped attract a few new/different kinds of guys.

The next day, after a particularly stressful day at the office, I parked myself in front of the screen and looked for responses. There were a few. After deciding not to answer the fellow who said he fell in love with my incredible arms and would love to have me wrap them around different parts of his body, or the guy who said he is a video game master and invited me to join him on a video adventure, I found an answer from a guy who looked reasonably attractive and sounded like a normal person. He lived in upstate New York. And he was my first online "almost date".

I learned all about the little tavern he had built off his living room, his two sons in the marines, his dogs, I liked that about him, his gorgeous cat, I liked that too. Didn't like that every conversation seemed to end with him telling me he had a hangover from "drinkin a few beers too many" the night before at the bar he had built and was so proud of. He also told me more than once that he had a "kinky sense of humor and did I enjoy that kind of humor?"

He didn't wait for me to answer.

He gave me some examples. Ugh.

Our flirtation spanned a couple of weeks of talking online. After a while I realized this was not a viable direction to be going in. Too many red flags, he crashed his car while we were in contact with each other, and all those proud referrals to his "kinky" sense of humor complete with "material".

And so, onward, fast. I had broken the ice by talking to Steve, I checked my Match email to see who else had popped up.

Then of course there was Peter the Pickle Man who you have already met.

The next couple of men I met were as wrong for me as Peter had been.

Mr. Harvard: the small business owner with the overly inflated ego because of his ivy league background. After a dull first date he demanded I not date anyone else or he was not interested. I figured after a month he would lock my house door and put a tracker on me when I went out.

Walter the "Weeble": His picture was way more flattering than he was in person. Pleasant enough. But when the waiters are standing behind your date, laughing and winking at you, you know this is not exactly a hot number.

Claudine, Darby, and I discussed "Peter's pickle, Steve's kinky sense of humor and the rest, over a great sushi dinner. Finding the funny is what made dating ok, and often amusing.

I did feel like a teenager sneaking around though, since Claudine and Darby were the only ones who knew what I was up to.

FAMILY LIFE REINVENTED

Starting over in the dating world wasn't the only starting over happening for me. The adjustment to being a family of 3 instead of 4 was rough. Every family has their own dynamics and when 25% of that dynamic disappears, everything feels wobbly, until you adjust to the new normal. That was going to take a long time. Marty might have been 25% of us but he occupied a way bigger part of our family dynamic. He was big hearted, loud, and opinionated. He ate too much, stressed too much, drank too much. He didn't do anything small. But he was also the teddy bear we could always rely on to make us feel safe in a crazy world.

When Lizzie would have any sort of illness or fear she would call Marty who would always tell her there was nothing to be afraid of, all would be fine. She would sleep easier; all was right with the world according to Marty. Never mind that Marty had some weird opinions we accepted as truth, because it was Marty saying it. Now there was no Marty to call in the middle of the night when a boy broke her heart, or she thought she was developing a strange and exotic disease. Marty's sister Linda has the kind of practical and calm mind that has been helpful, and Lizzie has taken to calling her sometimes. But much as Linda is calmer and more reasonable than her brother was, sometimes she is almost too practical to take Lizzie's issues seriously enough.

Robbie and Marty always had sports to bind them together. Hoops in the driveway, softball games played together as Robbie got older, and hours and hours of cheering on their Yankees and Giants. As a lifelong Yankee fan, I tried to fill those shoes, but I was a sad replacement. I grew up an only child and since both of my parents have been gone for years, Marty's siblings and their families are all the family the 3 of us have. The silver lining was we banded together even closer.

My kids saw me in a new light, more aware of my quirky sense of humor and my take on life. When Marty was alive my kids and so many people in our lives had trouble seeing past the combined Marty and Molly blended persona. I was always the "wind beneath Marty's wings" propelling him forward and helping him believe he could accomplish things he never thought he could. Now I was being the "wind beneath my own wings", and Robbie and Lizzie were beginning to understand what made Marty call me unsinkable Molly.

In the darkest days after Marty died the 3 of us could make each other laugh with some sick humor. Like thinking about cause of death on the death certificate.
"Chicken bones!"
"Mom that's not funny."
"It kind of is."
"Dad would even think it's funny Lizzie."
"Uncle Jerry says it was Daddy's fault he shouldn't have gone back for seconds behind Mommy's back"
"I actually saw him coming back to the table"
"Why did he always treat me like a Mommy he had to hide stuff from?"
"Cause he was a big kid."
"The biggest…"

"Remember when he paraded around the neighborhood playing his bagpipes on St. Patrick's Day?
"It was 9 in the morning on a Saturday, I don't think people appreciated it."

And just as I was trying to get back on my feet and find a new relationship for myself, Robbie and Lizzie were trying to pick up the pieces of their own worlds. Lizzie's years long relationship with a saxophone player had fallen apart right before Marty passed away, and Robbie had been without a girlfriend for a couple of years. Both were ready to start looking for love again. The 3 of us were on the same page, but what I learned the hard way was, even though Marty was no longer here, neither of my kids wanted to hear about "my page". They were supportive, they were happy I was going to date, in theory. They wanted me to be happy, and they knew Marty would have wanted me to be happy too.

I remember the first conversation we had when I told my kids that I was thinking about dating.
"Mom, that's great! Dad would want you to."
"Yeah, he used to tell me that if you lived longer than him, he wanted you to find a nice guy to torture just like you tortured him. You know his sense of humor Mom."

"Yup. But I know he meant it. "
"Just make sure whoever it is doesn't have crazy kids"
"Yeah, no crazy kids please."
"And no right-wing nut jobs."
"Do you think I would date some Maga monster"
"Not on purpose…"

"I wonder what Dad would have thought about all this…"

"You mean the election? Dad might not have liked far left liberals, but he was disgusted by the far right.

And he hated Donald Trump. Dad did some work on that golf course of his, and never got paid."

"Yea, no Maga guys Mom…"

And so, we were all busy on dating websites. They were swiping left and right at the same time I was looking for love on Match.com. How bizarre is that??

But until there was someone serious for them to HAVE to learn about, they wanted to stay totally ignorant of my "adventures". This took a couple of blunders for me to figure out. I thought we were all in the same boat and could share, insensitively forgetting I wasn't their buddy I was their mom, and in their minds, I was putting someone else in their dad's place.

Finally, one night at a girls' night book club get together I told the Mom Squad I had taken the leap into dating. Specifically, online dating. They were fascinated. They wanted to see my profile and the guys who popped up. I couldn't blame them for their curiosity. This had all been as foreign to me as it is to them. But I was starting to believe I had a right to a new beginning. Losing Marty was the worst thing that had ever happened to me, But I was at the point where I felt I should at least investigate what my new life would offer, which was a way to "do dating" differently. I was only 21 when I met Marty. I had only dated boys, and I was naïve. Now I had life experience, maturity and I wanted to experience it in a new way.

THE FRIENDLY POLICE OFFICER:

Clay Hill the police officer, 12 years younger than me was the first person I met that I shared with the Mom Squad. Nice profile pictures and once we started texting, I learned a lot about him. He was a devoted son, and a devoted father to his one daughter. His Mom was in and out of the hospital and he was there for her. And then the texting turned to getting together and Clay displayed another side…

I mentioned that I had two very loving Bassett hounds, they like to kiss people a lot.

"Oh baby," *(he loved calling me baby, even though we hadn't met yet.)*

I love to kiss too…how bout you?

"I do, holding hands is a particular favorite thing for me. It's the little things."

"Ah yes baby. You need my kiss too baby"

"Hmm sounds interesting."

Clay then suggested:

"I think we should kiss when we meet, before we even say hello."

"Interesting. I keep my clothes on when on first dates though."

(I had only had one first date in this chapter of my life, so this is true.)

"A sensual kiss. How about the 2nd date? Clothes come off?

"Not generally, but I'm worth waiting for."

(Was this ME talking??)

"Want to kiss you so sensually soooo bad."

"I'm blushing"

"When I meet you for dinner no words just kiss when we first make eye contact."

This should have set off danger bells for me, but I had been chatting with Clay long enough to believe he was harmless. Then he sent me a picture of himself without a shirt on, and his head cropped off – just his very muscular chest.

(Maybe it wasn't his chest??? But if it was....WOW!)

"It's all yours baby"

"Can I have it with a shirt on for the first date please. It will give me something to look forward to.

It was definitely at least worth meeting up. It was a VERY nice picture.

This story was too funny not to share with the Mom Squad (minus some details of our texts) who were intrigued as hell. Then their protective bells went off.

I was meeting up with Clay at a restaurant about a half hour from our homes in Tarrytown. Halfway between his home in upstate NY and mine. They wanted to follow me there.

"Molly, what if he is one of those online predators?"
"We should follow you."
"We'll keep our distance, he'll never know. We'll wear disguises."
"Guys you don't need disguises, he doesn't know who you are. But no need to come…I'll bring pepper spray."

That comment helped. The ladies backed off. And no, I did not bring pepper spray. Sorry ladies if you're reading this, I told a white lie.

I get their concern, but I was going to jump outside my comfort zone this time around.

I met Clay outside of the restaurant, and we did kiss. Hot concept. In reality? Eh, not so much. Clay ended up being a sweet, not very smart guy. And it did seem that it could have been his chest in the picture… It was a fun night. We even made out like teenagers in his car after dinner. That was something I hadn't done since I was like 19. And THAT was nice too. We texted for a while, talked about a second date. But it was obvious to me, and I think to him, this was a one and done adventure. We were from two very different worlds.

Felix, the rock concert promoter:
Divorced and now living with his mother in Chappaqua (*the rock promoter part was sexy, the living with your mother at 60 years old not so much*) Felix took me out twice. On the second date he started kissing me on the couch in the bar of a restaurant I frequented. It must have been one of my sexy new shirts with the cold shoulders that made him think it was ok. I could have pushed him away. But he was a good kisser! If one of my kids or friends had walked in, I think I would have gone into the witness protection program, but it seemed like a good idea at the time.

On date 3 he showed up at my house instead of meeting me at our chosen restaurant as we had discussed. I was taken aback, but let him in. It was a nice enough night, but he was getting way too amorous for me, which is why he probably took a chance and just showed up at my door. I just wasn't that into him. I knew when I pushed him out the door (*in a nice way, but literally pushed him*) at 11 that this would be our last date.

Navigating this new path was confusing, but I was getting some unsolicited help learning when someone was wrong for me…from Marty. If I was on a date and the guy was a definite no thanks, I would "see Marty "standing behind the guy. Sometimes he would be rolling his eyes. Sometimes he would be laughing. Sometimes he would just be mouthing the word "no". Crazy? Maybe it was just my subconscious talking. Whatever. His "presence" was helpful.

I was also gaining a new vocabulary attached to online dating. *(Of course, by now everyone has probably heard these words, but it was all new to me at the time – and I experienced every one of these things.)*

Breadcrumbing:

Breadcrumbing as you may know, but I did not back then, means you're leading someone along, usually by sending text messages occasionally. I learned that if I was getting flirty messages from someone who *seemed* to like me, but the texting went on and on without a date on the horizon…I was being breadcrumbed. One guy even told me that he was new to this, and he now saw there were so many options, (like choosing ice cream flavors I guess) he didn't want to jump at taking a chance on me.

Catfishing:
Romance scammers I found out, use this technique to con lonely people out of large sums of money. They build a

"relationship" by gaining your trust and affection online, sometimes for months or even years, but it never leads to a face-to-face encounter.

Meanwhile, you'll be asked to cover emergency expenses, invest in 'opportunities', help them flee a foreign country by wiring funds, etc. If someone you're messaging *always* has a reason why they can't meet in real life, you're likely being catfished. I encountered but was not fooled, by quite a number of these scammers and have included my experiences.

Ghosting:

I know you've heard of this before; someone you've been texting and/or dating vanishes without telling you why. The ghoster stops replying to your texts and won't take your calls - it's like they've just disappeared, and yes, it sucks. And yes, it did happen to me.

And then there are just your run of the mill online strange online dating experiences such as my encounters with:

The Wine Enthusiast:

A widow with the beautiful smile who spent 5 years crying and making wine. He had a basement filled with bottles of wine he had made. The odd thing was when I questioned him, he hadn't really liked his wife that much. And he didn't like wine much either. He didn't drink it. He didn't sell it. He just kept making it. He told me there were hundreds of carafes down there and you couldn't walk in his basement. He even showed me a picture. I suggested…

"How about giving it away?"

"Maybe I will, what a good idea, maybe next year…"

The Cheesy Poet:

Henri (*not Henry – Henri*) We met on Match but coincidentally knew each other through our children's soccer teams. Henri was a widower, and in his mind a true romantic. Soon after we started chatting, I started receiving long poetic emails with way too much information and way too much Harlequin romance pronouncements of infatuation. Henri and I went out on two dates on the second one he showed up with a lovely potted plant for me. It looked a bit like one I had received after Marty passed. I was speechless. I did kiss Henri once. Big mistake. I received a ton of lust filled texts after that, and I had to very slowly find a way to say I was not ready for a real relationship. This would become my go to way of backing off, who knew I had to find such a thing??

The Comedic Magician/Accountant:

As much as these dates and my introduction to the world of online dating were entertaining in a way, they were not anything that was going to last beyond a date or two. Then I received a warm, silly Match email from Morty the accountant. Morty! Who is named Morty who is less than 90 years old? Morty is a down to earth, funny man. His emails made me laugh, and that was worth a lot in my book. Morty's profile picture was not very appealing, but I figured some people weren't photogenic. We started emailing, and he constantly made me laugh. I was in like.

We met for the first time at the clock tower in Grand Central Station. Morty looked a lot like his profile picture, unfortunately. When he saw me, he stopped in his tracks and said, "You're so pretty, I'm out of my league"" I'm out of his league???" I didn't know I was in any kind of league.

Morty treated me like a queen. He kept saying he couldn't believe I would go out with HIM. He was so nice to me. He took me to wonderful places. Top of the Rock. Beautiful restaurants. He brought me flowers at the restaurants. Gorgeous arrangements, that I once managed to topple over spilling water all over both of us. He did magic tricks to make me laugh. Sent flowers to my office *(which Darby helped me hide from the rest of the staff)*. He was such a total mensch as we Jewish people say. *(a "great person" in translation")* I was falling for the idea of how he treated me. I did kiss him a bunch of times. He was an ok kisser. But then I opened my eyes and looked at Morty. And Morty was, the right name for Morty. I couldn't picture getting all naked and cozy with Morty. At all.

But what a sweet man he was. Constantly concerned for my well-being. We dated for 3 months, and he always tried to check in to see if I was ok. One night I was out with Darby, and he called. Darby answered my phone and when Morty asked where I was Darby said…" Me lady is drinking buckets of wine, and snugglin up to the bartender." Morty demanded to speak to me. I was not "drinking buckets of wine" or snuggling up to the bartender" just Darby's idea of a joke.

Morty was so worried about my well-being he offered to come drive me home from Manhattan. A true gentleman.

But not the gentleman for me. I once again used that same break up excuse on a date a few weeks later.

"I wasn't ready." Morty said he wished he had met me a year later after I had gotten this dating adventure out of my system. I told him maybe that would have made the difference. It wouldn't have made any difference, but I'm glad he thought so.

When I think of Morty I smile and hope he is happy. I know he loves to ski and is a ski instructor on the weekends. I think of him in the winter months and hope he's met an adorable ski bunny who appreciates his kindness and humor. A divorced Dad who adores his kids and will treat the right woman like gold. I'm just not that woman. What Morty did teach me was there are good men out there. Men looking to find someone to love them, who they can love back. I have encountered so many women who believe all men you meet on dating sites are assholes, looking for quick sex." Not true. Maybe when they're 25 or 30 and life stretches out before them there are more people like that. At 50 plus, the realities of loneliness and empty sex have set in. There are lots of good people out there. You can find them, if you keep your eyes open.

NOT REAL. NOT FUNNY.

While I am an eternal optimist and see the good in people, online dating is like anything else where you put yourself out there, you must be smart about it. I learned a few things about this. For starters that "catfishing" term I mentioned is no joke. Some lonely women believe these dudes and that can lead to a broken heart, or the emptying of your wallet.

I encountered a few of these characters. I ended up speaking to a few of them over time – always on those quiet nights when I would be sitting alone with just Sheila and Estelle for company. I considered it interactive entertainment, more interesting than watching "The Bachelor".

My "favorites" were the ones that had an identity, disappeared off the site for a couple of weeks, and then I would see their picture with a totally different name. They generally had come to America from Europe, from their profile info; the stories were colorful and sad. Their wives had died in an earthquake or in childbirth and they were left to raise their special needs child by themselves. Or…they owned their own airplane company and flew back and forth to Europe to make sure they could check in on their ailing parents. (*Therefore, you are led to believe that they are fabulously wealthy…so when they ask you for money you believe it's just a momentary need.*)

They were always filled with compliments. They fell in love with your picture. By email two they were sure you were unlike anyone they had ever met. They wanted to make wild passionate love to you on a beach, a mountaintop, and to treat you with the kind of special love you had never experienced before. Then they would disappear for a bit and reappear saying they were in dire need of funds to help their parents, their cancer-stricken child etc., so that they could return to America and make you their woman forever.

There was one "troll" who I spoke to a few times. I would flirt with him. He would complement me. I don't think he was one of these Europe based guys. Just an American brand of the same thing. It did let me brush up on my quick repartee skills. In case you've never actually experienced anything like this, here are a few of these lovely gents that I encountered.

This first man had a handsome profile picture. Too good to be true. This is the first email I received from him outside of the website:

Dear Sara Lee, *(of course not Molly)*
My name is Brent Smith. Background – Father – Irish. Mother – American. Am 55 years of age. Widower with 1 son. Body type athletic. Height 5'11'. Eyes Blue. Hair – Black
(What am I buying a horse – this is already weird)
I have a clever, quick witted sense of humor. I don't smoke. Drink occasionally. Born and raised from a Christian background, Conservative. I like dining, outdoor activities, travel, cooking camping, reading, watching sports. Computers. Internet. Playing sports and lots more. I am a nice man seeking for a caring woman and honest woman to spend the rest of my life with. I am looking for a

woman that is tender hearted, kind, considerate of other's needs. One that would appreciate having a husband that would love her in a way that she's not been loved before. I am originally from Edinboro, Scotland but I live in Bridgeport, Ct, USA. I am a successful businessman into buying and selling gold, diamonds, and gems stones. I am new to this internet stuff, and I want you to know that I am not on here to hurt anyone, and I don't want to be burned too. I just want to settle down and meet that special woman to spend the rest of my life with. You sound like a very cool and nice lady and will want to know more about you. I will want to know what you seek in life. I'm quiet kind, loyal. A great meaning for me is a human's soul. Circle of my interests is various. I like literature, music and cinema, personality traits are calm, honest, kind, loyal flexible elegant, sociable, sensitive, gentle, cheerful, optimistic, and very romantic. I am very understanding, open minded with a heart of forgiving, loving, and caring with sense of humor, hard working with cheerful character, honest, sincere, kind warm and intelligent with good look.

Will be waiting for your email. My pictures are attached below.

Stay blessed.

Brent Smith

This was my first experience with these scammers and my antenna said there might be something wrong with this, but the picture was soooooo gorgeous. We emailed back and forth. Brent's adoration for me grew exponentially. By email two he was calling me his beautiful brown eyed queen. At first, I was right there with him. Hey, this guy knew a good thing when he saw it! Then around email 4 Brent's son had a tragic accident and was in the hospital.

All of Brent's money was tied up in gold and gems. Could I help? Fortunately, at this point I thought I would show "the man of my dreams emails to Claudine and Darby.

Claudine immediately said – "English isn't his first language"
"Yes, it is. He's Scottish."
"No no mon cheri. Look at how he constructs his sentences."
Darby chimed in – "What a wanker!
"He's out for your money me lady."

My vision of sailing off into the sunset with this "romantic dreamboat" sank. I sailed off into the sunset and stopped answering his emails and eventually the emails from Brent stopped. About a month later I saw Brent's picture up on the dating website again. Except now his name was Frank Hoffman. Frank's story was "I'm divorced for 7 years and was married for 20 years. But I had to file for a divorce when my ex cheated on me while I was away in Australia working for about 6 months. I have a 21-year-old daughter who is currently studying at the Oxford University in England. I now work with an Oil Company in Texas, but I retire next month. I currently work from home but until I am retired, I can be called back into work anytime I'm needed. Who knows where Brent/Frank is really from? Perhaps he's just a guy in Tulsa, Oklahoma making it up as he goes along to make a living off poor lonely women.

Another one of these guys contacted me and asked some interesting questions:

"What's your turn on's and turn off's?

Do you have any tattoos and body piercings?

Out of curiosity, almost always late at night when I couldn't sleep, I would read these profiles. They were always "seeking a serious long-term relationship and more". They listed their wonderful attributes and asked for yours. The "business model' was always similar, they would ask more about me, compliment me, fall in love with my picture and my wit. My wit usually went right over their heads because they either didn't speak English well or weren't paying attention. They were busy plotting out next steps.

One of my favorites was a guy who "met" me and then went out on an oil rig and "missed me desperately". I was safe in my living room, and that was the beauty of it. If you don't fall for it and send these losers or fake people money it can be amusing. BEWARE! And that is Molly's public service for the day.

VERY BLIND DATES

While I laughed at my experience with Brent, it did make me think about taking people up on their offers to fix me up with the "really lovely guy they just knew I would love". I took a sabbatical from my evenings at the computer and went on those dates. That's how I met:

Maurice, the restaurateur. Nice enough guy. Friend of a friend. Maurice was a widow, for 5 years and I was his first date. Over dinner he told me how amazed he was that I was able to be out there dating after a year and a half.

This would be a sweet story, but when I questioned Maurice about his late wife, he told me their marriage had been loveless for many years. I wondered how long it would have taken him to go on a date if he had been madly in love. It also made me wonder what he thought of my ability to "get out there again" as he put it. I somehow didn't believe him when he said he "admired me". I bet he thought I had no moral fiber. Maurice did have a lovely smile though, which is why I agreed to a second date. Date 2 was no more inspiring than date number 1. Maurice had an amazing depth of knowledge about the quality of vegetables in restaurants. Fascinating. But how long can you talk about brussel sprouts? It was on date number 2 I experienced that Marty appearing thing. I "saw" him standing right behind Maurice, mouthing the word "loser".

I also went on a date with a lovely plumber friend of one of my Mom Squad girls. Philip was a nice guy, but when he walked in my friend had neglected to tell me that yes, Phil had been doing great on his diet. He had lost 15 pounds. He just had to lose that other 95. I was afraid he might crush me if I ever got to the point of getting up close and personal with him. Once again, I decided to steer my own ship, and if that meant encountering a few fake people online it was still better to take it into my own hands.

THE "EDUCATOR"

Not long after my blind date disasters I encountered an intriguing profile online. Handsome picture. Articulate profile with just a hint of arrogance. Nobody's perfect right? Arden Lane was his name. Such an interesting name, right out of a soap opera. I boldly took charge and emailed him. I had decided this was a necessity if you don't lie about your age. It's all about the algorithm and who says what age they are looking for. Mostly men my age were looking for somewhat younger women.

After my second flirtatious, and I thought witty email, Arden responded. It turned out that on top of being quite attractive, Arden was fabulously wealthy. His father had made a killing in the tobacco market *(so to speak)*. That should have sent me running in the opposite direction since I had refused to take on a tobacco account in my PR working life. But handsome and rich? Why not? I wasn't marrying him.

Three times divorced Arden lived in a giant house in Darien, Ct. not far from Tarrytown and yet a whole world away. His home was the cleanest home I had ever seen, with a squeegee hanging in every bathroom and instructions on how to keep the glass shower doors clean printed and sitting very neatly on the bathroom counters. Everything sparkled. There wasn't an animal or a plant to be seen. And the couches were all white! I just knew that nobody ever ate anything outside of the kitchen or dining room. I believed Arden was 4 years younger than me, according to his profile. Silly me, he had lied on his profile and was 6 months older. He became intrigued with me because of my boldness, and he thought I was pretty, although he constantly reminded me that he had never dated anyone as old as me.

I spent 3 months dating Arden. He gave me one amazing gift. He brought me back into the world of the sexually living. The first time we kissed he told me "That is one amazing kiss you're packing lady." That puffed me up. After a few dates when I took that first step of having sex with someone other than Marty, he was quick to point out that after all this time I was "like a virgin again" which he found intriguing but bazaar.

Arden who deemed himself a "very sexual man" was my teacher. He did have a lot of skill in this area. Clinical. Bossy. But enlightening and helpful for future use. It was not unusual to spend most of a Saturday in bed with Arden... *(I would elaborate but Lizzie told me if I did, she would NOT be speaking to me again for a very long time)*

Anyway, this was a learning experience for naïve, long married Molly. I would probably have broken up with him sooner if not for that.

To be fair, we were mismatched from the get-go. Arden would tell me I needed a nurturing guy, and he was not that. He's right but the way he said it I know it was not meant as a compliment. But does that mean it's okay to walk away from your girlfriend in bookstores and chat away on the phone for half an hour at a time. Or to throw hissy fits when your train shows up 10 minutes late and he must wait for you to arrive and feels inconvenienced?

One of Arden's other interesting quirks was he insisted I pay my own way on just about everything, because he had a hang up about women only wanting his money and about running out of money *(I guess when you have like 20 million dollars that's a thing?).* We took some interesting trips to Newport and Martha's Vineyard in his private plane, and he asked me to contribute for gas to fly the plane. And that was on top of insisting I pay for my own dinner most of the time. I didn't mind doing this, it was just the way he went about it.

He also had an incredible temper and only seemed to want to do what he wanted to do, which is probably what led to his 3 divorces? After about the 10th time that he insisted I pay for my own dinner I got up and left the restaurant. That was the end of Arden. I will always be eternally grateful to him for the education though.

OVERSHARING

I did make the mistake again of including Robbie and Lizzie in what was going on in my life. They were underwhelmed at the idea of me jetting around on a small plane with some "rich arrogant jerk". When I first mentioned it, I was a little blinded by the glamor of the trips *(we were in the process of planning a trip to Europe)* And then there was also my newfound sexual awakening. It was at this point in my life I came to terms with "my disease". I am a dyed in the wool "oversharer" and need to find a cure. I regaled my kids with the excitement of my adventures *(not the sexual parts)* and was at first totally blind to the fact they were not only unimpressed, but they were also pissed at me for telling them.

Lizzie had started dating a lawyer who moonlighted as a stand -up comedian. When I met him, I was thrilled to find that his offbeat sense of humor was helping her lighten up and laugh more. And he just loved her violin playing!

Robbie was another story. He was dating a hair stylist, gorgeous but not real interesting, in my humble opinion. I hoped she wouldn't last. But I was glad they were both moving on with their lives.

The Mom Squad was a whole other thing. I shared certain things, like my adventures with Arden. I told them, in way too much detail about ALL my adventures. with him. Which led to some memorable conversations about Brazilian versus bikini waxing – and who did which, and the answers to that question were surprising.

My life was now so vastly different from the life of a 30-year married woman. While this made for some good laughs, it wasn't the smartest thing I could have done. You just don't need 5 of your closest friends "in the bedroom with you". They wanted to know more. My kids wanted to know less. The lesson here? Keep things to myself!!

I also made the "mistake" of sharing too much about my latest online "friendship" with a tall handsome man from New Hope Pa. Matt and I started texting and talking on the phone soon after I stopped seeing Arden. Matt was smart and seemed very kind. He was a widow with two grown kids and did a lot of charity work. Matt had been widowed for several years and his desire for a partner to go through life with was oozing out of him. Matt called and texted me every day for 4 weeks. *(Including a couple of over the top "hot and heavy sexy phone calls to me while I was sitting on the train. This should have set off my warning bells, but it was kind of fun.)*

Matt was fascinated by my job, my interests, and my family. When he sent me two dozen long stemmed red roses on Valentine's Day Nancy said "Whoa that's kinda out there. You haven't even met yet."

Nancy was a little different than my other Mom Squad friends. She was the only one who had divorced, dated online, and remarried. She was way more knowledgeable about how this stuff worked. Instead of heeding her very intelligent comment I became defensive. "Nan, stop treating me like your little sister. I know what I'm doing here."

"OK…ok….but I'm worried."

Matt invited me to spend a fun filled day in Manhattan with him. New Hope was a distance and he wanted to give us lots of time to get to know each other. I got off the train and there he was, all 6'4' of his handsome self, waiting for me with an expensive piece of jewelry and a "surprise for me". He proudly took me by the hand and brought me over to a wall outside of Grand Central Station where he had written our initials in chalk. At this point I started to get uncomfortable and once again saw Marty standing there rolling his eyes and mouthing the word "crazy". Having invested weeks of chatting with Matt I decided to ignore Nan and Marty and threw myself into enjoying the day.

We had lunch at a mid-town restaurant. Then we went to a Broadway musical matinee. Fabulous orchestra seats. Halfway through the show I started getting this weird feeling as I started seeing many "Martys" up on the stage, shaking their head as in "NO, NO, NO". For dinner we went to a very over the top fancy French restaurant where Matt started stroking my leg under the table. When we walked out of the restaurant, he grabbed me and started kissing me. Not a bad kiss, but it must have been fantastic in Matt's estimation because he started shouting: "Game over, game over!" As in, now I was totally his. I was looking around hoping no one heard him. Matt then grabbed my hand and said he had one last surprise for me.

"Surprise? There have been so many already Matt, how about we save it."
"Nope you're gonna love this."

Matt grabbed a cab, and we ended up on Central Park West in his brother and sister-in-law's penthouse apartment.

They were waiting for us with champagne to have a toast because they had heard so much about me.

This was Crazy. I talked Matt into having the evening end after this and we headed back to Grand Central.

On the train ride home, I thought about what had just gone down and texted Nancy. "Nan you were right. This guy is a first-class crazy stalker man" The next day I knew I had to end this ASAP. After one, although expensive first date, I thought a long carefully worded text would do. I used the gentle "I'm not ready for a commitment "approach. This did not go well. Matt was mad. "I expected better from YOU "He texted.

For several days I received angry texts about how I led him on…or how we were meant for each other, so he thought. He tried multiple approaches. Finally ending with how his friends had told him that he comes on too strong all the time. This was a lonely guy who had let his imagination get the better of him because we had great phone/text chemistry. My thought was "Wow, this was after one long date. How would he feel if you broke up with him after a month?" I had ducked a big problem. I owed Nancy a big apology.

MY BORDERLINE PERSONALITY LATE NIGHT FRIEND

I made one "friend" whose name was Ted Kennedy. All my cautionary bells should have once again gone off. Ted Kennedy? Really?? But Ted Kennedy was only 42, good looking and, according to him, a news producer for one of the big networks. He did have an email that was attached to that network. I believed it all. Now I think maybe there's a way to do a fake version of a work email? I don't know. But my ego was so pumped up…

Ted Kennedy and I ended up chatting and flirting a lot after 11 pm. He could be highly articulate and interesting, then suddenly, a switch would go off in his head. He would obsessively start insisting I send him pictures of myself. *(I should have started considering the fact that Ted might have a major personality disorder at this point)*

"Ted, you have seen pictures of me – they're on my profile."
"That's no fun, I want BETTER pictures. "

I sent him a picture of my big toe and asked if that was good enough. Obviously 'better" involved certain parts of my anatomy.

This little flirtation went on for way longer than I am proud to admit, a couple of months. In my defense it was late at night, and it beat watching Jimmy Fallon or Kimmel or Colbert. We graduated to facetiming. He was a real person. Great looking and so normal, right up until… he wasn't. Looking back, I am now SURE he had a personality disorder of some kind. At the time I was too busy refining my flirting skills. Teddy would make dates with me and then cancel. I did meet up with him for drinks one time and he was very insistent on going back to his place, within about half an hour. I said no thanks and went home.

On my way home, I got a text of him with a naked picture, which wasn't all that impressive. I told him NO THANKS. He responded by saying "c'mon this is fun." I think Teddy didn't really like connecting with people, only pictures. I have since learned this naked picture thing isn't that unusual on dating sites – but NOT something I was going to be getting involved with.

After this he made one more date with me. Not sure why I said yes. He stood me up. I sat at the bar in a midtown restaurant in shock. I had never been stood up in my life. I stupidly let him start texting me again a few days later. *(What an idiot I was!)* He apologized profusely by telling me his mother died. I spent the next two weeks consoling him.

We lost touch a short while after that. Only to have him try to get back in touch with me 6 months later. He sent me a picture from a vacation he had taken with his sisters, nephews, and his MOTHER!

I would be lying if I said these late-night chats with Teddy that spanned over many nights did not fill a hole in my life. The fact that this younger, good looking, professional *(I think, who knows?)* guy (*ok crazy*) was interested in me was exciting and totally outside the world of a 59-year-old, long married lady. I felt young again.

Teddy did give me a few tips about profile pictures and things that were interesting. He helped me see the perspective of single men. He might have been crazy, but some of what he said made sense.

I still wonder if his name is really Ted Kennedy (*doubtful)* If he is a tv news producer (*prob not)* And I'm glad his mother isn't dead.

OUCH!

A lot of my friends would ask me how the dating thing was going. My upbeat attitude had given them a rosier picture of what it is like to be single and dating online. Rejection was a part of it. My friends thought I hadn't dealt with this much, based on my sunny attitude. But rejection is always part of dating whether you're 16 or 60. You're gonna break a few hearts and you're gonna get your heart, or your pride, damaged at some point. There were plenty of ouchy moments. Starting with guys who would "ghost" on me, it can be very confusing. You have great texting conversations for like two weeks, you seem to have a lot in common. Plus, there is all this witty and flirtatious back and forth. Then suddenly, nothing. That happened to me, more times than I like to remember.

Then there was this stiff CFO type who I found out on our date had 6 children who lived in another state. He proudly told me women kept throwing themselves at him. In fact, he had a date before and after me THAT NIGHT. He jumped up brusquely after an hour and said, "We are not a match." *(Thank goodness for that)."*

Nobody likes to be rejected. I much prefer doing the rejecting. But at least with this form of meeting people you don't have to deal with them after the fact. I would dust myself off and move on.

Moving on is obviously harder to do when you've invested some time into a person and think there are possibilities between the two of you. For me the best example of that was Bradley Winston, an attorney who seemed to be gaga for me, in the beginning. We had several romantic dates that included dinner out in downtown NY followed by drinks in the outdoor garden on the roof of his apartment building. And included some kisses under the moonlight up there *(very bad kisser – but the whole setting made up for it, maybe?)* And the romantic texts, every night at bedtime. All so wonderful until he came to my house and was underwhelmed by my cooking skills and the smell of Estelle's breath as she drooled on his lap. He also seemed to be less than enthusiastic when I told him how much fun it could be to spend a whole day in bed. This comment was fueled by my recent "awakening" by dating Arden. His response was "fun…or fatal."

After this "lovely evening "together he slowly but surely stopped texting me. I should have reminded myself that we would not have been a great match. Bradley Winston was the epitome of one of those preppy frat boys who I hated in college. So good looking and arrogant. So wrong for Brooklyn born Molly. Bradley was also extremely proud of his massive vocabulary. There was more than one time that I had to look up the words he used on google while he went for a bathroom break.

Then there was the fellow who told me he saw me more as a friend. How he saw me that way so fast – like before we even went on a date mystified me. A while after this I saw him on the train platform with what looked to be the morning after an overnight date. The lady was obviously 15 or 20 years younger than him and me. She looked like a high fashion model. They were barely talking. But talking wasn't really the point.

STAN THE NICE, TRIVIA GENIUS MAN:

After a while I could even laugh at the rejections. All my crazy adventures kept me laughing, but if I hadn't met my share of good, real people I would have given up. Yes, there were crazies out there, but plenty of good people too. One good person I met I still stay in touch with. He became a friend.

Stan is a realtor in Maryland. We started talking online and he was so nice and REAL. But Maryland? So far away. I crazily suggested we meet for the day in Philadelphia. He liked that idea. Our day together was so nice. We took in all the tourist sites, the Liberty Bell etc. From then on, we had a late-night conversation every night for a few months. Stan was a trivia buff, and we would play trivia. He always won, but I did learn a lot. Stan came up to my place for a few weekends. The first one he told me I was way too trusting. But my natural instincts were correct. Stan was a perfect gentleman. We always had a nice time. Long walks. Dinners out. Movies on TV. When his mom passed away, I helped him through it. Stan had two grown kids who lived down in Maryland, and I had my twins here. Neither of us had any intention of moving, so Stan said he knew this would not last. He said to me…" I know it's just a matter of time before you meet Mr. Right and remarry." I told him he was crazy. But eventually our relationship faded. We do stay in touch from time to time. Recently he told me he thinks he might have found "the one". I hope so!

TIME GOES BY

Marty had now been gone almost two years. I could think of him "in the big picture" without crying. But when I would think of the small moments, Marty's pride over his artistically shaped pancakes, his silly dancing, goofy made-up songs, his kilt and bagpipe performances, and ridiculous impressions of famous people, those are the memories that still hurt so much. I kept moving fast, to outrun the pain. The running did keep it at bay, but late at night, or driving and waiting at stop lights, having coffee by myself in the kitchen we used to share, the pain would slap me in the face. Grief is a huge adversary, but I refused to let it knock me flat on the ground. The tears would come from what seemed like a bottomless well. Then I would push back, get up and keep going. There would never be another Marty. No one who would give me Marty's huge bear hugs. Hold my hand with Marty's warmth. Sing me made up songs all about unsinkable Molly. But there could be someone with new specialness. New ways to experience life together.

My dating time so far had taught me there were people out there who were intelligent, attractive, with specialness of their own. It just had to be the person who's "special" connected with mine at this time in my life. And I needed to invest a lot more in realizing life as Molly, on my own two feet, could be cherished all by itself.

I started volunteering at the local animal shelter. I had always loved animals. Always had at least one dog or cat. and sometimes a bird, a fish, a hamster, even a ferret. My career and raising the kids had stopped me from pursuing volunteer work. Now I had the time and I walked through that door. Inside those animal shelter walls, I found "my church, or synagogue". I found new people I could share a common goal with, to give these lost furry souls the love they deserved before they found their forever homes.

Annie and Mary ran the shelter, and two nicer people you couldn't meet. They "adopted" me, and I found a whole new purpose. I threw myself into the many ways I could help. I walked dogs. Socialized cats. Cleaned cages. And I got involved in dog training to help make dogs more adoptable.

On any given day you could find me hand feeding a giant pit bull to teach him food bowl manners, taking dogs into the pens to exercise them, running orientation classes for new volunteers. The list of possible ways to help was long, and I loved it all. And when one of the long-time doggy residents was adopted into a perfect home I celebrated with my new "family" at the shelter.

Even Lizzie and Robbie got involved. Both started volunteering with me. On holidays we got up early to go to the shelter and help the staff do their chores so they could go home and enjoy the holidays with their families, since there are no days off in shelter life. The animals always need to be walked, fed, and loved. We all developed our favorite animals. It's a miracle we haven't ended up with 12 animals in my house. I asked Annie how she kept from doing this: "I tell myself that if I brought home say 12, there would be another 12. So, I spread my love around, and try not to hyper focus."

"But what about when you fall in love, sometimes it just happens…"

"Then I focus on finding that special love a home."

"Aren't you sad to say good-bye?"

"Yea but I feel so happy for the family and that special animal."

I took this advice to heart and Annie and Mary trained me in how to be an animal adoption counselor. I also decided that while my cat sanctuary idea might have been over the top, fostering kittens in the shelter's kitten foster program might be fun. And what a treat to be caring and nurturing for another being, instead of having people taking care of us. As much as the support of friends and family had been essential, I have always been an independent person, able to care for myself. I was eager to get back to feeling capable.

Lizzie had just broken up with Mr. Stand- up Comedian and was looking for something to occupy her time and she pushed me to get involved.

"I'll help Momma. "

"Okay they really need help now. So many babies that need to be socialized."

Lizzie and I brought home our first kittens to foster. Two months old and hissy and scared. They slowly stopped hissing and started purring and sitting on our shoulders like little monkeys. We loved it. That experience emboldened us to try and help save the youngest babies that come in without their mothers. Days old, these little kittens need to be bottle fed like newborn human babies every few hours. I was hesitant to take it on because I work all day in the city.

Lizzie convinced me our opposite schedules, since she worked in the theater at night, would make this doable.

Lizzie moved back into her old room for a while, and we took in two one-week old kittens. We named them Peanut Butter and Jelly.

Right from the start it was obvious little orange colored Peanut Butter was way stronger than dark striped Jelly. We fed and nurtured them like they were human babies.

One day about two weeks after we took them into our homes, Lizzie called me at work, crying.
"Momma Jelly isn't…. isn't"
"Isn't what? I can't understand what you're saying."
"Isn't breathing…"
Poor little Jelly didn't survive. I came home, and Darby came with me.
We put Jelly in a little box, had a service for him and buried him in the backyard.

Darby recited Hebrew prayers for Jelly as the 3 of us sobbed together. Peanut Butter thrived, thank goodness. After the trauma of losing Jelly, there was no way Lizzie was giving her up. She was a ball of orange fluff, and sooo sweet.

Lizzie moved back into her apartment taking Peanut *(shortened for everyday use)* home with her.
Robbie was not as excited about this as we had been. While he had nothing against cats, he was still dating

Astrid the hairstylist. Astrid is allergic to cats and Robbie was pissed.

I went over there with Lizzie when she brought Peanut back to her place.

"Lizzard you suck!"
"I love you too Robbie."
"You KNOW Astrid's allergic."
"Actually, I didn't know, but she doesn't live here I do."
"C'mon I KNOW you don't like having her around."
"I never said that."
"How is that being a good sister. When you were dating Bart the bad comedian I laughed at his stupid jokes."
"Actually, you rolled your eyes half the time."
"But the other half I laughed."

I quietly snuck out of the apartment leaving them to work this out on their own. The way they "worked it out" was Robbie started staying over at Astrid's most of the time. This didn't bother Lizzie one bit. It made me sad. These two have a bond only twins understand. As different as they are, they understand each other. I was hoping this wouldn't put a long -term wedge between them.

STRANGER THAN FICTION

Time went by. My company was chugging along, but it did take a fair amount of my brain to keep it going, and the rest of my brain was given over to my kids, the shelter, and my friends. But I've always had a lot of energy, so there was still plenty of time for me to wonder where, when, and how I would ever find love again. I would take breaks from searching and then find myself wandering back to the computer. And the "stranger than fiction" experiences kept coming. Online dating was still kind of fascinating at this point because it was such a bazaar experience, but after a year of it, my patience with the weird stuff was beginning to wane.

For instance, there was Steve. I had a date set with Steve at a very nice restaurant, and then Robbie happened to show up at the house in the evening when I had the computer on. Steve's profile was on the screen. Robbie screamed: "Mom why are you talking to Drew Thomas?"

Huh? "That's Steve, I can't remember what his last name is."

"Ma that's Drew the gym teacher where I teach."

"He said he's in real estate."

"Side gig Ma, and he's too young for you…"

"He's 47…"

"Wrong 42!"

Now this was a new one on me, someone who is lying UP about his age???

And not saying what he does for a living!?

"Wow, this is strange…why would he lie…"

"Why is your name Sara Lee?"

"Good point…"

"So, what's the big deal…"

"Ma, he lives in this weird old house with two of his siblings, none of them are married.

I'm glad he's into older women since he works with kids, but NOT MY MOTHER! We call him 'Woody' and I'll let you imagine why.

I started to think about my conversations with Steve/Drew and yea they could get a little weird… pleasant, nice …. but then he would excitedly start asking me about my lingerie and tell me what he would love to see me wearing, in detail.

I cancelled the date. Robbie breathed a sigh of relief.

I did think I had developed a good system for staying safe. I had a few ground rules. If I didn't know someone's last name, I wasn't going to even meet them for a first date.

I shared my first and last name too to demonstrate my commitment to fairness. I had gotten very accomplished at "google espionage". I would check men out before I met up with them. Then If I did go, I would relax and be myself.

There were a few times that "google espionage" saved me from some uncomfortable situations later.

There was Mark, great looking picture, pleasant to chat with and he kept refusing to give me his last name.

I kept refusing to meet for drinks before I knew what it was. Mark finally relented. I did my background check and found that Mark was a long-established Scientologist,

(which is certainly his right, but as someone who doesn't even go to Synagogue, I thought Scientology was beyond the fray for me)

Mark also had some very kinky videos on his YouTube page. When I broke the date with him, Mark was furious.

"You are a hypocrite he said. I tell you what you ask and then you don't want to meet me!"

"I'm so sorry, please forgive me but I don't think we would have much in common."

After calling me a bunch more names and swearing at me Mark disappeared into his Scientology world.

There was also a city official who I found on the local tv station who was under investigation for embezzlement. Okay so "innocent until proven guilty" but I figured why go there? While my friends would fret over my safety, I didn't take it for granted. I was on the case. But even being cautious didn't always keep it from getting just plain weird. For instance, when I was messaged by someone who at first glance was my kids' age and at second glance, I realized was in their third-grade class. This was no fake scammer. This was just a young man with a major mommy complex. I messaged him back that he should try and find someone a decade or two closer to his age. And NOT the parent of some past classmates of his.

Then there was Nick. Nick was a widow, according to his profile and had two small grandchildren. Nick was a few years older than me. Good, he's truthful I thought. On our second date Nick mentioned his divorce. What divorce I asked. Turns out Nick had been married for 30 years and his wife died. He got involved with another woman and lived with her for a couple of years. They married and she threw him out and divorced him within 4 months. Strange. That was a couple of years before our dates. But Nick was still hurting. He then happened to mention her full name. Sandra Shultz.

"I knew a Sandra Shultz" After a bit more discussion we figured out that Sandra was my first cousin. The child of my dad's estranged half-sister. We had not been in touch with this side of the family for 25 years. I said "Nick, I can't date you. I can't date my first cousin's ex-husband."

Nick however felt even more interested in dating me based on this new information. He thought it would be great revenge to make sure Sandra knew he was seeing her estranged first cousin. Nick had also told me in his quest to find the right woman he had been on many, many first dates. Hundreds of them. A second date meant you were on your way to the alter. But not after our second date. Nick was on his way out. Door closed and locked.

Then there was Richie who clapped to congratulate me over everything I was doing with my life, after practically everything I said. We happened to be having dinner at the bar of a restaurant and when Richie got up to go to the bathroom the couple across from me looked over with sympathy and the woman said, "Bad first date?"

I laughed and said, "How did you guess?" I was beginning to think I was winning the prize for most bazaar dates ever. I was losing patience, and then…

TEENAGE CRUSH TIMES TWO

Then I met a couple of men that made me feel like I was on the Bachelorette and "falling for more than one man". I kept all this to myself, but my kids could tell there was something going on. I heard Robbie telling Lizzie "We should lock her in her room."

Of all the nerve. Who was the mother here?

Maybe I was acting like a teenager, but I had just been hit by lightning. A full out crush, blinding me to the reality of the absurdity of the situation. Searching through the dating site I had chanced upon Jay Thompson. A video editor and rock musician. Jay was ten years younger than me, and to my eyes, gorgeous. I was in lust just looking at his picture. His hair was on the longer side. He had a cute little earring in his ear, He was so young looking, so hot, I boldly messaged him. He messaged me back. He found my boldness "adorable".

We set a date for dinner. Jay walked into the restaurant, and I almost fell off my chair. When he came over to the table, I wanted to ask him if he had the right table. How could this gorgeous hunk be interested in ME???

He was mesmerizing. Jay sat down and after I regained my ability to speak, we ended up having the most amazing 3 hours. Time flew by. When I told him what I did for a living we realized we could have even worked together…

Jay said "You've worked with editors and still want to speak with me? We can be anal and perfectionistic."

"Doesn't the drummer in a rock band even that out?"
"You are one smart lady."

Jay kissed me good night in the parking lot, and I did the most uncool thing possible. I was so overwhelmed I walked straight into my car door. What a dork. But he thought it was charming.

Jay and I texted and spoke constantly after that. I also cheered him on when he played at local bars with his band "Extreme Sport."

We watched movies together, including what I called "50 shades of silly" instead of "50 Shades of Gray". Jay thought it was hot as hell.

I told him "I don't like rules. I'm all about the gray area. Which is probably why I have such badly behaved dogs."
To which he responded, "Perhaps you need a little discipline."
Jay made me laugh. A lot. He made me feel great all over.
We took long walks on the beach. He made a heart out of big rocks on the beach for me.

He even wrote a song for me called "One So Strong" all about being forced to start over, with lines like "After thinking that she was weak she was the one so strong."

My crush kept escalating. Never mind that he had two sons aged 7 and 13. As one of the Mom Squad who knew about this mentioned…

"Do you really want to start all over with two young kids?" I couldn't even think that far.

All I could think about was Jay made me feel young and desired. He was constantly telling me how he was going to crawl in my bedroom window. And I couldn't wait.

So, you may wonder…did he ever "climb in that window."

Some things a girl keeps to herself. *(According to Lizzie as far as her mom's life is concerned).*

After two very nice months I could sense Jay pulling back.

He told me he still hadn't gotten over his girlfriend. *(Not his wife, that was over years before)* Said girlfriend who was 20 years younger than me. Jay said, "I am very grateful you have come into my life. But I'm struggling to find some harmony between my head and my heart. I'm not sure I should be dating at this point".

"Now you tell me. I thought we had something special"

"We do. I just don't want to use you as an emotional band-aid Molly."

"Use me...just kidding."

"I need to work on my mindfulness"

"Get mindful fast, then call me. Don't close this door…"

"I close no doors…just need time."

I believed him. Jay was a good guy. True to his word he did contact me when he was ready a few months later. But I had moved on. Every few months Jay would get in touch again. Too late. Our timing was way off. Our stages in life were way off too, so I guess it was for the best. But I'm glad I got the chance to get to know him. He taught me that even at 59 years old magic can happen.

Fortunately, magic did enter my life again, the right magic, when I was ready for it. While I was seeing Jay, I was messaged by an attractive man who looked like he was half African American, Jonathan Landy. He proudly stated he was African American and Caucasian/Jewish. African American and Jewish? I could make my mother happy and piss her off at the same time. My mother had tried all kinds of manipulation to get me to marry a Jewish boy, including telling me that on my grandma's death bed her one wish was that I would marry a Jewish man. An utterly ridiculous statement since my grandma was the opposite of her spunky daughter and never tried to push anybody around. Sadly, for my mom I never seriously dated anyone Jewish, maybe because she was so intent on me doing so. Shirley wasn't a big fan of Marty's at first. Over the years his big warm hugs and silly sense of humor won her over. The good story on my mom is that she was a sucker for a good joke, particularly if it was at her expense. Marty was relentless in his mother-in-law jokes. Telling her since she was all but 4'6" tall she was going to have to sit in a car seat in our car and taking her on in games of Scrabble where their equally mercenary competitive spirits would lead them to cheat constantly.

JONATHAN PART ONE

Jonathan Landry was intriguing. And HE pursued ME. Handsome, but with a shaved head. *(I really like a nice head of hair, so this was a stumbling block.)* But he had an interesting profile, an internist who was now a full time Educator at Columbia Medical School. Divorced with one grown son.

I still had Jay very much on my mind but thought I would at least get to know a little more about Jonathan. We started texting. Unlike so many of the men who had contacted me Jonathan was not a flirt. He was straight forward and nice but not a flirt. I had gotten used to that flirting thing, so I was a little disappointed. Looking at old texts to write this book I was a little yucked out by all those flirty texts. Jonathan was also not into texting. He asked for my number after just a few texts, and we had a first phone call.

Jonathan had this deep mesmerizing voice. It made me think of an expensive pinot noir, or a great cup of hot chocolate.

That first call we shared a little about our lives, enough to decide we would meet.

I only shared his profile with Darby. No one else.
"This mate is NOT a wanker Moll…"
"Doesn't he seem a little…. dry."
"No, no, he's just honest. Real. I know these things…"

Jonathan suggested we meet at his favorite local pub, which oddly had been Marty's favorite as well. Perhaps this was fate?

I walked in and Jonathan was seated at the bar. I poked his shoulder, he turned around, and smiled at me with one of the warmest smiles I've ever seen. His eyes crinkled at the edges in the softest, sweetest way.
"Hi Molly, nice to meet you."

I would be lying if I said lightning struck on that first date, but Jonathan was easy to talk to. There were no games. Just honest conversation. We shared our stories. He was both sympathetic to my situation, and able to laugh at the ridiculousness of the dark comedy attached to so much of my life.

His story was interesting. Jonathan was born in New Orleans to his African American Dad and Caucasian Mother. His parents met while attending Tulane University, married, and had Jonathan, their only child. Growing up in a mixed marriage in the South was not always easy but Jonathon thrived. He loved the food and the music of the town. He finally left to attend college in upstate New York, at a small, "little ivy school" Union College, near his mom's hometown of Albany. Jonathan was a pre-med student. While he was there, he met Kara who would become his wife, a beautiful, 6-foot-tall brunette who would go on to become a lawyer.

Ultimately Jonathan claimed they both worked too much and became strangers to each other. They were very similar, intense people. But when Kara ran off with an airline pilot he was devastated, even though their marriage had long been missing its spark.

Byron, their only child, was a freshman in college at the time. Kara moved to Florida with the pilot and Jonathan was left with a lot of time to think about what had driven them apart. He decided to lighten his work pressure and became a full-time professor of medicine at Columbia University.

He had dated over the last 13 years but hadn't found that special someone. He was almost at the point of giving up hope after so many bad dating experiences. In fact, this was his last week on the dating site. And he had found my profile the week before.

"What made you reach out to me Jonathan?"
"Your profile had a refreshing lack of bullshit.
 Even your bathroom counter shot looked like you were out of your element."
"Hey, I was very much in my element!"
"Ok if you say so...."
That first conversation was enough to make me want to see him again. I was fascinated by what it must have been like growing up in New Orleans with his mix of heritage.

"It's not as weird as you think. Jews and African Americans were both not exactly welcome at Mardi Gras when I was a kid. BOTH sides of my family were outsiders.... that makes you kind of on the same team. Ever hear of the Krewe du Jieux?"
"Is that a Passover recipe?"

"Nope just their version of Mardi Gras dress-up and throwing bagels instead of coconuts."

"Interesting. I've never been to New Orleans. So even Mardi-Gras itself is foreign to me."

Two hours later we agreed to have dinner the following week. I slowly started to see the person underneath the pleasant exterior.

Jonathan loved all things New Orleans. New Orleans jazz. New Orleans cuisine. He was proud of his Jewish background AND his place as an African American from Louisiana.

Jonathan's Mom was a member of the Touro Synagogue. I was surprised to find out there was a vibrant Jewish community in New Orleans, even though there were only 12,000 Jews living there. Touro, a reformed synagogue, was one of the first synagogues in the country. As a reformed temple it was the right place for Jonathan's Mom who had married outside her faith. The rabbi had been very welcoming to Jonathan's Dad and growing up as part of that temple had been a great experience for Jonathan.

This was also the start of my education about all things Creole. My stomach needed some adjusting, but it was interesting. My favorite moment early on was when Jonathan asked me "Do you like to cook?" and I answered" I can cook a decent one-hour recipe but I'm just as happy not to."

He very pleasantly answered: "Good because I would just piss you off." Jonathan had a very specific palette, and it involved all things I would call "Creole light" He loved the food but as a doctor he was way too educated to eat totally that way. So, he preferred his own inventions. I found out that was fine by me. The food was interesting but cooked his way it wouldn't add 200 pounds to my waistline.

Jonathan and I began seeing each other regularly. But Jay was still in my mind. Then, on our fourth date I walked up to the restaurant and saw Jonathan sitting on the terrace of the restaurant, sun shining on his face as he spoke with Byron on the phone. For the first time it hit me how handsome he was. I think I was afraid to see it before. It was also on this date he kissed me for the first time. For a man who had never even flirted with me, that kiss was a gamechanger. The big thing that started coming through was that I had never met a man anything like Jonathan. He was masculine and sexy and yet there was no "frat boy/bromance" stuff in his being. That was refreshing.

After our date I was driving home, and Nan called me. I told her about our date, and our first kiss.
 Nan said: "I think you're starting to have real feelings for him…"
I was not ready to admit this.
"Nan, are you crazy? He's not my type. And his wife broke his heart."
"Mol, his wife is remarried and that was over a decade ago."
"Right…. right…. But the cultural differences. Where do I fit in with his family in New Orleans?"

"Where did you fit in with Marty's big crazy Irish family? Every relationship brings its own set of players and challenges."

"True…we shall see…."

Jonathan and I continued getting to know each other. As a Jewish woman you would think that parts of his background would be familiar to me, but his Bar Mitzvah story was only slightly less foreign to me than his New Orleans food choices. I had never been Bat Mitzvah-ed and he knew more about our shared faith than I did.

He was such an interesting blend of his cultures. On the one hand he occasionally told me he would light candles for the Jewish Shabbat, but then on the other hand he loved unkosher southern cooking.

Our first trips to the supermarket together were strange. Jonathan kept putting things in the cart that I would never think of eating and I just went right along with his choices, like I did at first with Marty. It would be a very slow process to find a happy medium between our two palettes and how to blend as a couple without losing ourselves.

After all these many months of finding out who I was on my own I was determined to keep track of my individuality.

I worried about whether Jonathan was getting to know the whole me. I told him this. He met serious Molly first. We talked and talked and shared our life experiences, and our souls, and the conversation came so easily. What about the fun parts, the silly parts? Would Jonathan like these parts?

He was such an intellectual. I really needed him to be able to be silly with me. It was hard to tell because the biggest issue was Jonathan could be warm and available, and then this giant wall would go up. This protective shield that he had developed to keep from getting hurt again. He became a little…robotic.

The first time this wall came up to smack me in the face was at a very big moment in our relationship. It was right after Jonathan spent the night for the first time. It had been a wonderful night. We had taken a long walk under the stars, eaten take-out sitting on the floor in my den. And Jonathan didn't seem to mind Sheila and Estelle staring at us, waiting for food to drop on the floor. Being together felt so comfortable. It felt like we were made for each other. It was so perfect that it scared the hell out of Jonathan.

A few days later when he was supposed to come down for the evening Jonathan was half hour late and no word from him. I gave him a call and he didn't answer. Then I called again, and again. He finally answered and his voice had a frenzied quality to it.
"I think maybe we should take a break."
"Why? That's insane."
"I, I just don't know if I'm ready for all this…"
"All what? I thought we just had a nice time together."
"Right…all that."
"Jonathan you're talking crazy. Just relax and let's have some fun. Get in the car and come here."

There was silence for a bit too long….and then Jonathan said…

"Maybe in a week or two."

I was totally stunned. I didn't see this coming…

I knew Jonathan had been looking for a real relationship over all the years since Kara left. But when it was staring him in the face he panicked. I was having my own inner turmoil. I had thought this was real. And that deepened my feeling that I was cheating on Marty. I had shared this with Darby, and her reaction was so her.

"Me lady Marty would be celebratin that you're back between the sheets."

"Darby c'mon…."

"Didn't he always say that if he died you would have an affair with that romance novel hunk Fabio?"

"Well…"

"Marty loved you and would want you to get out there."

"Speaking of getting out there Darby, what's happened with your many men?"

Since Terry, her husband had disappeared while out getting a newspaper, Darby had made it her business to have one boyfriend who was the main guy, and one as back up in case the main one disappeared. I had pointed out that this might keep her from ever getting into a lasting relationship again. "I'm doin just fine. And then there is my perfect mate, in Afrique." I had heard about this perfect mate for a couple of years now, and Darby had begun talking about going back there.

Getting back to Jonathan and me, the fact that Jonathon had basically run away like the runaway bride would have been even more distressing if I wasn't having some cold feet issues myself. I was hurt. I was angry at him. But maybe he wasn't right for me? Maybe this was for the best. I distracted myself with extra time at the dog shelter, trying to refocus on my business. And I took a break from looking for any other new men. Maybe I was just fine on my own.

JONATHAN PART TWO

Two weeks went by and just as I was beginning to think Jonathan was history, I came home to three dozen roses sitting in front of my front door. I said aloud…" There must have been a fire sale at the florist."

I took the flowers into the house, and Jonathan drove into my driveway a half an hour later. He knocked on the door and asked hesitantly:
"Any interest in letting me in?"
I said: "Maybe, let me think about it." Then he knocked again.
"How about if I promise not to be such an asshole ever again."
"Ok I'll let you in, but only if you promise to tell me why you think I should."
"Open the door and I'll tell you."
Jonathan said: "I don't know what happened to me, I panicked. I had such strong feelings for you, it scared the hell out of me."

But then he said he kept thinking about how I hadn't reacted pissed-off and accusatory. The fact that I was understanding, and non-threatening made it easier for him to show up again.

That was the start of a new phase. Molly and Jonathon as a committed couple. As I spent more time with him, I was able to act silly without fear he would think I was an idiot, and I was able to coax the silly out in him. It started the day I came down dressed for a meeting with two obviously unmatched shoes. The heels weren't even the right height. Jonathan thought this was hilarious.

Then there was the time we watched a movie called "Ghost" not the one with Demi Moore and the potter's wheel. This was a newer movie, an arthouse flick. I found it goofy. Jonathan had studied film and loved these art house type films. There was this ghost, which was just a guy wearing a white sheet who had gotten stuck in a deserted house and was sadly living there waiting to be set free. I went to my closet and got a nice white sheet and chased him around the living room. I had never heard Jonathan laugh so much.

We also started discovering each other's little quirks. Jonathan loved music. He loved to sing but was embarrassed to let anyone hear his voice. I loved hearing him sing the blues in the shower, or while he worked on his computer, at the top of his lungs when he didn't know I could hear him downstairs in my house. As an amateur drummer he also used absolutely everything as a drum and would grab any kitchen gadget he could find as a drumstick.

He found my style of picking up piles of papers and moving them from one place to another to "clean up" way more endearing than Marty had. He also had a calming effect on me. Jonathan never raised his voice. An argument with him was more of a discussion of the issues. We had very constructive arguments, unlike Marty and I, who would scream at each other, then hug…leaving us still in love, but nowhere near fixing the problem. With Jonathan the opposite was true. We analyzed things, sometimes to death. While this was great in some ways, it also took a lot of getting used to. Sometimes I would ask him if he was a girl. He wasn't fond of that and told me that was extremely sexist of me.

I had been in one relationship for so long that many things were just second nature. In a new relationship the good part was it was all new and exciting. And the bad part was, it was all new and anxiety provoking. I had to get used to a whole new way another person did things.

I wanted Jonathan to feel safe that he could talk, and I would listen. So often Marty and I would get frustrated with each other. And then say we were never on each other's side since we had some major disagreements about things like religion and politics.

Then there were just the everyday little things. Marty had been very sloppy, leaving a trail of clothes from the living room to the bedroom and dirty dishes always in the sink. Jonathan was totally opposite. His closets were so neat and well organized it made my head hurt. I was a firm believer in keeping my home tidy, but no one should ever look in my closets or under the bed. I committed myself to being more organized with my closets and shelves, with varying levels of success. Jonathan kept telling me that we balanced each other out.

I didn't walk into this new relationship understanding on a conscious level that a new relationship is work. But I am a fast learner. We had to learn how to eat together. Sleep together, like what side of the bed? He likes hard pillows. I like soft. He washes the mattress protector every week. I wash it like once every few months. And that was all just in spending time together enjoying each other's company. Then there was interacting with other couples? What would this new thing called Molly and Jonathan be? And what about our families? How would they feel interacting with us? And our friend.

JONATHAN AND MOLLY... AND THE WORLD

First meetings with our kids were, of course, the ones we cared most about. I had been careful not to introduce Rob and Lizzie to anyone I wasn't serious about. And they had no desire to meet anyone who wasn't going to stick around either. When I told them, I was bringing Jonathan to dinner they knew this was important. Lizzie looked curious; Robbie looked like he had eaten expired yogurt. That first dinner set a pattern for what we would have to work through. Jonathan is good at bringing people out of their shells, and he asked Lizzie all about her musical career. He had personally seen "Phantom of the Opera" 3 times and had probably heard her wonderful violin playing the last time he was there. When he told her about his love of New Orleans jazz greats like Louis Armstrong, Jelly Roll Morton, Wynton Marsalis and Harry Connick Jr., and his drum playing hobby she lit up further. They talked so easily. Robbie on the other hand sat there with a snarky look on his face.

The next day I asked Robbie. "I thought you wanted me to find somebody and have some happiness."
"Yup, I do Mom."
"Then why the nasty bulldog act?"
"I can't explain it. I'll try better next time."
I get it. None of us had expected there to be anyone but Marty at our table ever. But I had come to terms with the fact that life happens, and I knew Robbie would too, in his own time. His heart was in the right place. I was grateful for that.

First dinner dates with friends proved challenging too. Many of my couple friendships were on automatic pilot after years of sharing so many experiences. We were so tightly wound into each other's lives. Friday night dinners out. Holidays away together. Movies, theater, kayaking so many shared experiences. They were expecting whoever I was with to fit right into this. And I did too, at first. The reality is everything was going to change drastically. It had to. There could be great new ways of interacting that we didn't have before, eventually. But it couldn't be the same. Jonathan was a totally different person. And Jonathan and Molly were a different entity than Marty and Molly.

My women friends were supportive. A few of the men not so much. They seemed to feel acceptance of Jonathan was disloyal to Marty. They missed him. It was going to take time. At first, I was hurt and confused. One of Marty's friends related a story to me about telling his mom, after she was widowed, that no man was going to take his father's place at their family table. He seemed quite proud when he told me "It would be over his dead body." Wow! This guy just didn't see his mom as a woman, just as a mom. He thought he was protecting their family and lacked understanding of how lonely his mom might feel.

Marty's own family members accepted Jonathan with open arms though. They understood Marty would have wanted it that way.

Looking back on some of the bad frat boy jokes that were aimed at Jonathan, and the lack of interest in me having a new life I am more understanding now. They had all suffered a major loss as well. Marty had many close men friends, and his passing was a giant hole in their lives. If I stayed Marty's widow, without another man by my side, somehow Molly and Marty lived on. Now that I was bringing a very different man into the picture that fantasy would die. I have way more sympathy for the reactions I encountered back then in hindsight. But I was too overwhelmed trying to stay afloat myself to understand how anyone past my kids would feel.

Some people that knew me in both relationships asked how I seemed so happy with Jonathan; he was so different than Marty.

How can you explain that? It's a different time in life and needs change. What Marty and Jonathan did share was a high standard of moral integrity, kindness, and the ability to love with their whole hearts. Those were the important things for me. Everything else was window dressing.

Then there were all the other first experiences. Like weddings and funerals *(yes funerals, they are part of life, and deciding when you should accompany your mate when you don't know the dead person, but they may want you there for emotional support is a thing)*

Weddings were a new thing for me with Jonathan too. Marty did not dance. Except for slow dances. He would sit and joke with the other men who didn't dance. I had grown accustomed to dancing with my girlfriends. Jonathan loved to dance, almost a little too much. He was great at it. I felt self-conscious. I told him I had no rhythm.
"I beg to differ girlfriend. YOU have great rhythm"
"That's different."

"Um no you just have to loosen up, on the dance floor."

Jonathan decided to give me dance lessons. He would put on music and whirl me around the living room.

I'll never win "Dancing with the Stars." But I have improved.

Meeting Jonathan's friends had its own challenges because Kara was very much alive. When they told stories from the past, I knew Kara would someday be walking through the door and I would have to deal with a living, breathing, beautiful and accomplished woman. This was not something I had ever imagined in my life. But I learned how not to feel like a jealous lunatic when Jonathan's best friend Jeff, from college talked about the crazy adventures Jeff, Jonathan and Kara would go on. Jumping out of planes. White water rafting in crazy currents. Snowboarding on black trails. Oh my god I am NOT an adventure girl. I asked Jeff. "How does your wife feel about all these adventures. Does she accompany you?"

"Who Moira? Don't be ridiculous. She's too sane for that. She saved me from myself."

"Well, that's something…."

Jonathan said, "Don't worry Moll, I would never do those things now."

"Would Kara?"

"Maybe, she's fearless"

"Oh. How nice."

I was starting to really dislike Kara. And I hadn't even met her. She was too accomplished. Too beautiful. Too adventurous. I couldn't compete. This wasn't Jonathan's fault. This was all my high school insecurities reignited. Every now and then I would make a snarky remark about "Perfect Kara."

Jonathan would be puzzled. "I don't get it Molly. You're amazing. I love who you are. YOU are who I am with, and no one has ever made me feel so loved and understood. No one has ever made me laugh and enjoy life the way you do. I don't want Kara back. We weren't right for each other. I would always apologize and say, "I'm just being a girl." Until the next time I heard something wonderful about Kara. It made no logical sense. I was married to Marty for 35 years. And I didn't divorce him. Jonathan had to deal with the ghost of Marty everywhere we went in my world. At least in his world people knew he and Kara were not together out of choice. *(Ok, her choice, and that was one of my issues.)*

Both Jonathan and I had to deal with each other's long established friendships and all the talking about the past that we didn't share. As time moved on, I knew we would create our own memories with each other and with our friends. But it was hard at first.

My first meeting with Jonathan's son Byron went way better than I could have ever expected. I loved him right from the start, and he seemed to take to me. Byron has some similarities to his father, but he's way less guarded. Handsome and adventurous like his parents, but more down to earth. Byron and I bonded over our deep love of "The Office." Byron wasn't really a fan of New Orleans jazz. He was a huge fan of Taylor Swift, which made Jonathan a little nuts. I like Taylor Swift too, so we had that in common. Byron was a resident in pediatrics at NYU. Jonathan had told me this was a perfect fit for him, since Byron had always been drawn to working with kids.

Summer camp counselor jobs, volunteering in foster children's programs. The kids always loved him because he acted like a big kid himself, throwing them up in the air, acting out inventive stories and just having fun. Byron and I connected so well that Jonathan would kid that I liked his son better than him.

"Only sometimes Jonathan."

We started meeting Byron for weekly dinners. Our meetups with Lizzie and Robbie were becoming more natural. Eventually we decided it was time to have our kids meet each other. I can't say the first meeting went spectacularly. Lizzie's comment on Byron was. "Nice, but kinda awkward."

Robbie was still fighting the whole idea of this new life of mine, not on the surface but enough in his subconscious that he didn't act like himself. I was dejected, and a little exhausted by how much work this all was, but Jonathan was way more sensible.

"Did you think they would just be deliriously happy at the idea of a blended family?" I knew that not to be the case as Robbie had let me know he was not interested in being pushed into being part of "some forced, blended family".

Another first for Jonathan and me was taking trips to see both of our childhood homes. For me that was simple. It was just down the road in Irvington, NY. I hadn't moved terribly far from where I grew up. Shirley and Hal had decided to leave Brooklyn when I was 5 years old, and I had spent all my formative years right there. A trip past my house involved one afternoon. Jonathan already knew some of my childhood friends, because some of them were part of the group I call the Mom Squad. We were a close-knit group who had been together for sooooo many years. Which is what can make it even harder for a new man to squeeze into the picture. Jonathan tried not to complain, but every now and then when the old stories that even he had heard a few times were trotted back out, you could see the exhaustion in his eyes.

A trip to visit his first home in New Orleans was a way bigger deal. Our first trip away together. I had never been there, and I was excited to experience the New Orleans of my imagination and of my boyfriend's childhood.

Jonathan was excited to share some of his favorite restaurants and music haunts and to show me where he had grown-up. We listened to local blues at the Maple Leaf Bar on Oak Street. We walked through the art galleries on Magazine Street. And over dinner at a cozy little place called Vyonne's in the Warehouse District Jonathan gave me a little history lesson on the New Orleans of his youth – and how both African culture and Judaism had played such an important role in the beauty of New Orleans and in his own growth.

Jonathan was excited to show me the synagogue he had told me about and told me stories about how much of an impact the rabbi had on him throughout his whole childhood. I loved hearing how his dad had played there for Jazz Music Fests sponsored by the temple.

Jonathan also told me about how both Jews and African Americans had felt left out of Mardi Gras festivities and started their own celebrations. One was called the Krewe du Jieux, started in 1995 – they threw bagels instead of coconuts.

"Well bagels wouldn't hurt as much as coconuts, as long as they aren't stale." I said. We drove past the house where Jonathan had grown up, not far from the temple. I'm sorry that Jonathan's parents have both passed, as have mine. I would love to have met them. I was glad that I got to meet some of his oldest friends that he played endless hours of music, and baseball with.

THE TURNING POINT

It was lucky we managed to take that trip to New Orleans in the Fall of 2019, based on what would follow, the Covid-19 pandemic that shut down the whole world in early 2020. It would have been a long time before we could experience it that way again.

As paralyzing as the events were, in some ways we grew as a family. In the early Covid days Byron was working extra hours at the hospital. This was before testing, before vaccines, and Byron was out there on the front lines. He saw first-hand the devastation of this horrible virus. The people dying alone. He was fearless and worked tirelessly. And Byron got Covid. Not a mild case. One of those horrible ones where they were talking about possibly putting him on a ventilator. We all had heard the statistics about how many people who went on a ventilator ever came off one alive. Jonathan was beside himself. Kara was calling him every day, round the clock. We now had a shared cause, getting Byron better. I ended up speaking with Kara every day myself, filling her in on what was happening and to discuss what course of action should be taken.

Two weeks went by and slowly Byron improved. At that point his hospital team told us he needed rehabilitation for his lungs. Byron was sent to Burke Rehab Hospital in White Plains, very near my home in Tarrytown. Kara and Gary came up from Florida. They drove all the way. Staying in hotels where they were still open. Sleeping in their car when they couldn't get one. With hardly any hotels open and the anxiety of getting Covid in the ones that were open, Jonathan offered Kara and Gary the option of staying with us. It was the right thing to do.

They stayed with us for almost two weeks. It was strange at first. But we all put on our big kid pants based on one common goal, to help Byron get better. Slowly we stopped looking at each other as aliens. With no restaurants open, nowhere to go, and the fear of Covid hanging over all of us, we became "bunker buddies". We played what I now refer to with affection as "Couples Therapy Scrabble". In one memorable game, Kara spelled the word "Paella" then said.

"Jonathan, that paella we had in Barcelona was my first time eating it. Never had it that good again."

Jonathan said simply. "Yea."

Kara is not always so good at reading signals, and she continued...

"Wasn't that our honeymoon?"

At which point Jonathan added the word "poi" And said that was the inedible food he and Kara had on that hideous trip to Hawaii.

"The only couple who could have a miserable time in Hawaii."

Now things were getting testy.

Kara said, "Do you always have to be so negative?"

And it was my turn in the Scrabble game.

I spelled "Gefilte"

Gary said, "Is that an allowable Scrabble word?"

I was sure it was, but I looked it up just to make Gary happy, and it was.

I commented "My first boyfriend took me to his house for Passover and we all got food poisoning.

His mother insisted it wasn't the fish. She ate it herself again the next day to prove it, and she got sick.

Stubborn lady."

Everyone laughed and that broke the tension.

Later Jonathan asked, "Did that story really happen."

"Kinda, it was my mom who made the bad gefilte fish, she was pretty stubborn."

"Good one Molly."

We learned how to loosen up around each other. I began to see why Jonathan and Kara, who are both great people, made a very bad match. Both so competitive and sure of themselves. They ramped each other up, until they both wanted to explode.

We watched movies and argued over what to watch.

Jonathan picked art house films in other languages.

Kara picked awful horror movies which I refused to watch

Gary picked sports movies, *(which I kind of liked).*

I picked character driven stories and sometimes even rom coms. Everyone groaned but I know they liked them; they just wouldn't admit it.

Somehow, we managed to find things we all would watch without too many arguments. We all liked documentaries for one thing. We watched a lot of those. Nan was amazed by our living arrangements. You are living in the same house with Jonathan, his ex-wife, and her husband? That's crazy."

"Nan, it's so far from what I ever thought I would be capable of doing. But I LIKE Kara now. And I can see why they were wrong for each other. And that's helpful"

"You're better than me Moll."

"If you were in this situation, you might be even better, you just don't know."

Jonathan had long harbored plenty of anger for Kara's leaving. Kara had just been happy to find someone who truly made her happy. And THAT made Jonathan even more pissed off. Finally, there was peace. Byron was grateful for the lack of angst between his parents now. He gave me the credit and called me "the miracle maker" Nice of him to say, but Byron is the one that really brought everyone together.

When Byron was allowed to go home, he came to my place. Jonathan had been living with me for several months. I had the room, and I was happy to have him. Kara and Gary stayed for the first few days. If anyone had told me this would be my life I would have said, no way. But it was working.

Robbie and Lizzie started coming over. We were all stuck in because of Covid and we became a "pod". Robbie and Lizzie were forced to get to know Byron. Many competitive games of Battleship ensued. It was one of the "gifts" of Covid that those of us who were privileged enough to be safe and warm in comfortable homes could enjoy. Robbie would still fight the "blended family" analogy, but there was finally plenty of time on our hands for everyone to get to know one another. Broadway was shut down. Robbie was teaching from home, so was Jonathan. I was working from home. Byron was slowly getting back to himself, so he could go back to working in the hospital. This made for a lot of nights, and even parts of each day spent together.

Time moved forward and everyone started getting back to their own lives as testing and vaccines became available. Byron went back into the city and back to work.

Lizzie and Robbie went back to their apartment. Robbie was still teaching remotely. Lizzie was working on new music on zoom with other musicians. Jonathan and I were once again peacefully alone in our little world.

With the exception that the realities of my business problems kept getting in the way. Working through Covid had been challenging. Creating videos for clients on zoom was bizarre. Financially I was doing ok since Marty's partner in the contracting business had made me a very generous offer for Marty's part of the ownership. That was a relief. My business itself has been a struggle. We had lost our biggest medical PR client right before Covid shut everything down and getting new ones was next to impossible in this crazy environment.

To make matters worse, Darby announced she wanted to go spend an "unspecified amount of time in Mali." I was at a loss about how to replace her. She helped make the agency move. Kara had graciously offered to do the books for me. I took her up on it, for the time being. I began the search for someone who could fill Darby's very "big" little shoes. Darby, Jonathan, and I had a send-off dinner together. We had made dinners together a weekly date lately, and Jonathan and Darby had developed a nice friendship. One of the new things I learned about Jonathan through these dinners was his interest in Africa. The other thing I learned was after he graduated from college, before starting medical school, Jonathan had spent a summer travelling all over West Africa and had solidified a passion for the people and their plight. Jonathan and Darby's conversations were always animated, and I think they both learned from each other.

Jonathan would often say to me afterwards that maybe together with Darby we could come up with more formal ways to help over there. Maybe start a foundation for improved medical treatment? His connections in the medical world could help make this a reality. I loved the idea. Jonathan shared his thinking with Darby. Her excitement was like a volcano going off in that little pink head of hers. Someday…

Finally, the day came for Darby to take off on her travels.
"Don't go marrying that African lover of yours. I need you back."
"I'll be back. On me honor."

The months went by and Darby as she had promised, kept in close touch. She took me on facetime "tours" of the school where she taught English to the kids. She showed me the very humble little hut that was her home, with her sleeping mat on the floor, the truck she used to go pan for gold, and the bar, where she spent a lot of time, that looked more like a shack than a bar.

I loved when she was joined by "her kids" and I got to know her boyfriend Amadi a bit through these facetime chats. I began to understand better why going there was so important to her. Darby understood so well the feeling of being imprisoned by the culture you are born into. In West Africa she had found a place where she could use the gifts of her education and empathy to help the children and women who became like family to her.

All was well until the day I received a call from Amadi. It was hard to understand him between his accent and the tears. The two of them had been riding on his motorcycle in Sierra Leone. They had crossed the border to help a pastor friend of theirs with relief for the starving children there. This is something I knew Darby was deeply committed to, and no matter how many times I begged her to stop crossing the border because of the dangers in Sierra Leone, she was committed to helping there. They had made this trip many times. But this time was different. This time they didn't see the bus coming at them until it was too late. Darby's little body didn't stand a chance. She was gone. And ironically it had nothing to do with Muslim terrorists. A simple, horrible accident.

Devastated. Horrified. Nauseous. This couldn't be happening. Darby was too special. Too joyful. Too giving, and the least judgmental person I had ever known. I have never met anyone like her. I probably never will again.

Calling Lizzie was horrendous. She came over and we shared our grief and our love for that 5' nothing pink haired ball of energy.

The loss brought back so much of how we felt after Marty died. Darby was one of the most influential relationships in my life and Lizzie's. Now she was gone too. I felt like I had fallen back into that big black hole. But this time Jonathan was there to listen, to let me cry and to hold me. In the short time he had known her he had felt the Darby magic and was deeply saddened too.

A service was held for Darby at the orthodox synagogue she attended in Brooklyn. The rabbi read one letter after another from people who had been enriched by Darby's generous heart.

There were letters from her students in Mali. Children who she called "my babies". The kids she taught English and paid for their schoolbooks. She also helped them learn how to play. I had seen so many amazing pictures of little Darby. The one white face in this small African village. So accepted. So beloved. How this could have been possible in a mainly Muslim country that had no tolerance for Jewish people, and in small towns where no Caucasian people are to be seen remains a mystery to me. All part of the Darby magic.

Darby showed everyone there how to live life with exuberance and wonder. This one tiny pink haired Caucasian woman in a village of West African Muslims. One letter after another spoke of how Darby had been the best friend they had ever made.

Then there were the people on the Zoom call from all over the world. Not only her friends in West Africa, including Amadi, and the reverend who she worked with to help feed the children, and some of the kids who loved her. There were friends she had made on her many travels, and so many said exactly what I said, how she had changed their lives, inspiring them to believe in themselves and live life with joy and purpose.

Many of the women at the temple spoke of how she had encouraged them to reach for new goals and to see their own potential. Lizzie and I could relate to that because she had done the same for us. Repeatedly in my head I remembered her telling me "We are sisters. You are me darlin sister, from another life."

I think she was right.

Even though Darby had been in Africa for several months before her passing, the fact that she was no longer anywhere I could reach her hit me hard. I couldn't believe the world no longer had this amazing spirit walking the earth.

Replacing her at my company was a whole other issue. Kara kept doing the books and finally after a couple of bad hires, I found a smart young woman with lots to contribute. She would never be Darby, but I was optimistic about the possibilities.

TIME HEALS

I had lost Darby, and Jonathan had almost lost Byron. We had learned so much about how our relationship enriched us. The forced closeness and time spent together that Covid brought to us had also strengthened our bond. A few months after Darby passed away, we started talking about getting married.

I just wanted Marty's approval. I know that doesn't seem rational, but I set up a zoom appointment with Joe the medium. The day of my appointment I closed myself into my basement office to connect. Joe came into the meeting and abruptly, which is his way of starting a session asked,
"Who is Ruth?"
"My mom's best friend. Like my 3rd cousin – I called her Aunt Ruth."
"She's here."
"She was my favorite relative of all time. So loving and non- judgmental. The best person."
"Marty is here too."
"Does he know I'm thinking about...""
"Getting married? Yeah.
"He says he sent Jonathan to you. "
All those other dudes were never going to take you through the rest of your life. His words.
Ruth outlived her husband by many years?"
"Yea"
"She adores you and says that being alone wasn't fun. She put on a good face. But she doesn't want that for you.
Don't worry about what the world thinks. This belongs to you."
"I do worry…"

"It's nobody's business how long you wait to start a new relationship.

Marty approves."

"His siblings have been supportive too. They like Jonathan."

Marty says "Of course they are. They love you."

"Marty likes that Jonathan moved in with you."

"Really?"

"Your aunt is back now talking about shoes….

Sometimes I don't know why they speak about things at first.

Now your mother is here too, talking about shoes…. Do you still have Marty's shoes in a closet?"

"Just the ones from the day he died."

"Aaah. That why they're all talking about shoes. Get rid of the shoes. You're holding on to the death."

"Somehow it makes me feel like a connection to him still being here It was his last day."

"Let go of the death. Stop holding on to the pain."

"He was cheated from having grandchildren."

"He will be with them, watching over them. Those clothes you have from the day he died. That's not what he wants you to remember him by.

It's time to release the death and remember the life."

"I need to know he won't be mad at me."

"He's not mad. He's clapping. He knows this will be a new marriage. You've been through a lot of life. You can use that to build something good, something mature and special. It's time for you to embrace the future you deserve.

Everyone who loves you believes this."

The tears were flowing but it was what I needed to hear.

LIFE GOES ON

Things were changing a lot for our kids. Astrid had broken up with Robbie, saying she needed someone more intellectual. The irony of all this is I had been so judgmental about HER intellectual abilities. Turns out she had an MFA in painting and that was what she did when she wasn't being a hairstylist, since it's hard to make a living as a painter. I was gonna miss her haircuts, and her great sense of color.

Robbie started spending a lot of time with another teacher named Tara. A very nurturing soul. Cute too. Robbie cried on her shoulder for weeks. And then figured out there was more to her than a shoulder to cry on. Bart and Lizzie got back together, and they were doing way better this time around. With no comedy clubs to spend time in Bart put all his attention into his law practice and into growing their relationship together. My two kids were doing well. Miraculously they were all spending a lot of time together in that two-bedroom apartment and getting along. And Tara isn't allergic to cats, she loves them.

The world was upside down with climate change and the pandemic. But in my little world there was peace.

Byron had met a wonderful young woman named Aimee. Another resident in the pediatric department, Aimee is Asian. Her parents grew up in South Korea. But she was born here. She and Byron seemed so happy.

With everyone getting comfortable in their own lives Jonathan and I felt even more sure that now would be a great time to take the next step together. I started thinking about the details of it all. A second wedding. What do you wear? What do you do when you're a blushing bride of 61? We talked about having lots of people and that was too much work. Some people still weren't ready to see me taking vows with someone else, even after a few years. I fully expected eventually they would get there, but why rock their boat?

We talked about a smaller wedding and decided to wait until the Covid pandemic had become less of a constant danger. We spent a lot of time brainstorming and fantasizing about what a wedding would look like for us. We talked about a destination wedding - Nova Scotia. We considered Italy- too much red tape. Bermuda – we would have to worry about hurricane season. Santa Barbara? Charleston?

We changed our minds so many times. Then I suggested New Orleans. Jonathan loved that idea.

We planned a small celebration In New Orleans with our kids. The day was filled with New Orleans' best music, great food, and fun. Lizzie played her violin, joining Jonathan's childhood friends who played music for us that day. And Jonathan played drums.

Bart did a comedy routine, and even Robbie said Bart had upped his comedy game. It was great to see how far Robbie had come with Jonathan. They had developed a nice friendship. And he even complimented me saying "Mom, I'm so proud of how you have made a life for yourself "unsinkable Molly" has really been swimming along nicely."

"Thanks honey, but first I had to learn how to float, all over again."

As I was writing this book, I remembered this conversation and I reached out to both of my kids and said – how about "Molly learns to float" as a title. And for the first time they both said. "YES!!

A NEW HOME

Jonathan and I started thinking about where we would make our combined home. Much as I loved my house it was time for us to make a change. A new home we could create together.

Everything was on the table. Moving to New Orleans? Maybe I could open an art gallery? Take singing lessons there? Sounded exciting, but we eventually came back to finding another place in a different part of Westchester. All our children are here or in Manhattan. We figured eventually there would be grandchildren in the picture. Grandchildren that we would share. A blessing for my kids since Marty was not on the planet.

We needed a new home for this new chapter. Someplace different than Manhattan, Chappaqua or Tarrytown, the places where we had each lived. We started thinking about New Rochelle. I knew it from my college days at Iona and had always liked the city. I worried that it wasn't totally new, but Jonathan was ok with the fact that I had gone to college and met Marty there.

A diverse community that would be very welcoming to our diverse family. We started looking for houses that made sense for us. Two months after we married, we found a ranch house in New Rochelle with room for Byron, Aimee, Lizzie, Bart, Robbie, and Tara to visit.

My friends in "the Hood" thought I was moving to the moon. No matter how many times I told them that it was only 20 minutes away. Change is hard, for everyone. Once again, I was upsetting the balance of things. Adjusting would take time. But I was positive that eventually it would get better. I was blessed with so many wonderful people in my life and I would do everything I could to keep them close.

I had learned to look forward with optimism. No matter what life has in store for me in the future, I will keep standing tall. Sometimes I wonder – what if it was Marty who I had met at this point in life? Would it have worked? I know that I would be a better wife than I was throughout the years with him. I'd know what a budget was and might stick to it every now and then. I'd listen better and help him feel less lonely in our relationship. Then maybe he would have listened more to me. What we had was flawed but filled with love, much like any marriage that lasts for many years. I feel blessed to have been his wife.

Now I am blessed to be Jonathan's. Our life is rich and filled with the beautiful surprises life can bring if you leave your heart open. Jonathan and I settled into our new life together as husband and wife. While we had lived together for two years there was something about being married that solidified our commitment. We talked so much about what we could do to make our future together more meaningful.

ONE YEAR LATER

A lot has happened in this past year. From the time Marty died until now my life has changed more than it had in the 20 years prior. Bart and Lizzie announced they were expecting a baby. And then Bart asked me for her hand in marriage. What a comedian.

Jonathan and I have been busy setting up our new home, shopping for furniture together. A new experience with this man. Marty only cared that our dinnerware forks had four prongs, the rest was up to me. Jonathan had "his style", just like he did with everything else. I was getting used to being married to a man who had a better sense of design than my own.

We were not only talking about starting that foundation, now in memory of Darby, we were making plans. We scheduled a fact-finding mission to West Africa. We would not be as adventurous as Darby, we would stay in safer places, but we would have Amadi meet up with us to help us see the real picture. It would be the beginning of a new purpose Jonathan and I could share. A foundation in Darby's name. A way for us to blend with a new future, but bringing Marty, who loved Darby so much, and Darby herself along with us in spirit.

I had all sorts of dreams of how we could use all our kids' talents to help us with it in the future as well. We embarked on our first trip there together. As the doors of the plane opened in Mali and we started walking down the stairs, suddenly my phone started playing a recording of music I had made about 10 years ago. It was of Marty playing his bagpipes. I smiled. So did Jonathan. He grabbed my hand as we reached the bottom step to begin this new chapter. Love never dies.

ACKNOWLEDGEMENTS:
I would like to thank my draft readers, notably Jody Rawdin (my long-time art director/partner/brilliant creative and trusted "sister"), Jamie Graham (advertising friend author/inspiration, and generous sharer of knowledge) Marla Severance and Barbara Anson (smart professionals and dear friends). Their suggestions and enthusiasm gave me the courage to publish my first novel!

Cover design and book formatting: Courtesy of Dani Carlson, whose talent and kindness is very much appreciated!

ABOUT THE AUTHOR:
After a lifetime spent writing :30 television commercials, print ads and all sorts of collateral advertising materials in her career as an advertising creative director/writer, this is Diane Wade's first novel. She is hoping others will follow and has some creative ideas swirling around in her head, hopefully they will turn into more books!

Diane Wade's first novel is a fun, frank, and honest story of a woman whose life was thrown upside down at age 58, and how she managed to reinvent herself.

www.ingramcontent.com/pod-product-compliance
Lightning Source LLC
LaVergne TN
LVHW012024060526
838201LV00061B/4452